"You look…hot." His gaze traveled the length of her body.

The compliment sent a rush of pleasure through her. "Thank you."

"You know what that dress says, don't you?"

Sierra couldn't think straight—not with the heady scent of Beau's cologne swirling around her head. "Wh-what does it say?"

"Kiss me," he whispered.

They hadn't sat down to eat and already Beau was making a move on her.

Go ahead. Sierra had fantasized about kissing Beau for months. Did it matter if he kissed her at the beginning of the date instead of at the end? Sierra made a feeble attempt to take the high road. "My aunt's sitting a few feet behind the door."

Beau's gaze zeroed in on Sierra's mouth. "I'm a quiet kisser."

Short of breath, she whispered, "Prove it."

Dear Reader,

If you love rodeo, family drama and sexy, headstrong cowboys then Harts of the Rodeo is the series for you! In *Beau: Cowboy Protector,* you'll meet Beau Adams, whose recent falling out with his twin brother has made him more determined than ever to win a national championship in bull riding. Rodeo aside, Beau is feeling a little left out of the holy-matrimony club—his brother and cousins have all married and are starting families of their own. Then Beau finally catches the eye of Sierra Byrne and believes a trip down the aisle might be in his future, but Sierra has other plans that don't include Beau. After receiving a sober medical diagnosis, Sierra is determined to live life to the fullest before her condition prevents her from participating in the activities she's always dreamed of doing. Now it's up to Beau to convince Sierra that "marrying Beau" should be on her list.

Next month look for *Tomas: Cowboy Homecoming,* the final book in the series, by Linda Warren.

And finally, I'd like to give a shout-out to the talented authors in this continuity: Cathy McDavid, C.J. Carmichael, Roz Denny Fox, Shelley Galloway and Linda Warren. Keeping track of all the details in each book wasn't easy and I shudder to think of the hundreds of emails that passed between us as we plotted our stories, but we persevered and brought this series to life, even managing a few good laughs along the way. Thanks, ladies, for making this experience so much fun!

Marin

Beau:
Cowboy Protector

MARIN THOMAS

HARLEQUIN®
entertain, enrich, inspire™

Recycling programs
for this product may
not exist in your area.

ISBN-13: 978-0-373-75429-8

BEAU: COWBOY PROTECTOR

Copyright © 2012 by Brenda Smith-Beagley

www.Harlequin.com

Printed in U.S.A.

ABOUT THE AUTHOR

Marin Thomas grew up in Janesville, Wisconsin. She left the Midwest to attend college in Tucson, Arizona, where she earned a B.A. in radio-TV. Following graduation she married her college sweetheart in a five-minute ceremony at the historic Little Chapel of the West in Las Vegas, Nevada. Over the years she and her family have lived in seven different states, but they've now come full circle and returned to Arizona, where the rugged desert and breathtaking sunsets provide plenty of inspiration for Marin's cowboy books.

Books by Marin Thomas
HARLEQUIN AMERICAN ROMANCE

*The McKade Brothers
**Hearts of Appalachia
***Rodeo Rebels

To my grandmother Dorothy West… Grandma, you blazed your own path through life— rather than becoming a hairdresser like your mother and sisters you became a bookkeeper. And you raised several eyebrows when you set your sights on the lead trumpet player in a popular dance band. Socializing was a huge part of your life and I know you're up in Heaven dancing your toes off and swigging down Manhattans while listening to Grandpa Bud's band. Thank you for being such a wonderful grandmother to me, Brett and Amy and a patient, loving great-grandmother to Desirée, Thomas, Michael, Tylesha and Marin.

You will be forever in our hearts.

Chapter One

"Where's your better half?" Bull rider Rusty McLean stopped next to Beau Adams in the cowboy-ready area of the Sweetwater Events Complex in Rock Springs. "Duke was makin' a run at the National Finals Rodeo this year, then he slipped off the radar. He get injured?"

Beau wished an injury had sidelined his twin from today's rodeo—he was the only Adams competing this first weekend in October. He'd hauled Thunder Ranch bucking bulls, Bushwhacker and Back Bender, to the competition by himself. Duke, aka deputy sheriff had remained at home protecting the good citizens of Roundup while the Thunder Ranch hands had taken a string of bucking horses to a rodeo in Cody, Wyoming. Beau's father was off doing who knows what with his new lady friend.

"My brother quit," Beau said. In July, Duke had blindsided him when he retired from rodeo, leaving Beau to carry on the Adams' bull-riding legacy. He'd flipped out, angry that his brother had walked away from a possible world title when Beau had sacrificed so much for him. Beau had spent his childhood defending his twin when bullies had teased Duke about his stuttering. Standing up for his brother had carried into their teen years and when they'd reached adulthood, it

had become second nature for Beau to make sure that
Duke remained in the rodeo limelight.

"You're joking," McLean said. "Duke was ranked
in the top ten in the country at the beginning of the
summer."

"No joke, McLean. Duke's done with rodeo." Once
Beau's anger had cooled, he'd realized Duke had never
asked him for any concessions, which made Beau wonder why he'd allowed his brother to beat him in bull
riding all these years. He had no one to blame but himself for the tight spot he was in—not enough rodeos
left in the season to earn the necessary points to make
it to Vegas. Regardless, Beau was determined to sal-
vage what was left of the year by winning a handful of
smaller rodeos leading up to the Badlands Bull Bash
and Cowboy Stampede in South Dakota the weekend
before Thanksgiving. A first-place win would show
rodeo fans that Beau Adams was a serious contender
for next year's title.

"You're pullin' my leg, Adams." McLean stuffed a
pinch of tobacco between his lower lip and gum. "Duke
wouldn't throw away his points 'less'n he had a good
reason."

The sooner the truth got out, the sooner Beau's competitors would forget his brother and take notice of him.
"Duke's been bit by the love bug." At McLean's puzzled
expression Beau clarified. "He got married."

"The hell you say. I didn't know he had a girlfriend."

"It happened fast." Crazy fast. So fast Beau's head
still spun. Of all women to go and fall in love with,
Duke had picked Angie Barrington, a single mom with
a grudge against rodeo. She ran an animal rescue ranch
outside their hometown of Roundup, Montana, and a
few of her boarders happened to include horses injured

in rodeos. Much to Beau's chagrin, Duke had traded in a trip to the NFR for a ring and instant fatherhood.

You're jealous. Hell, maybe he was. There must be a bug in the water back home, because Duke and all but one of Beau's cousins had married in whirlwind romances reminiscent of Hollywood movies. It irked him that Duke was all in love and Beau had yet to catch the eye of Sierra Byrne, a woman he'd been flirting with since spring.

"Too bad about Duke. His loss is my gain," McLean said.

"Don't get cocky." Beau grinned. "You gotta beat me to win that buckle." Buckle aside, Beau wanted to take home the prize money—three thousand dollars. Not a fortune by any means, but with the tough economy, the cash would help pay a few ranch bills.

"Adams." McLean snorted. "You ought to know better than anyone that Bushwhacker's the best bull here. All I gotta do is make it to eight on him and the buckle's mine."

The braggart was right—Bushwhacker was the top-rated bull at the rodeo. At five, he was a year older than Back Bender, but both were money bulls. So far this season, Bushwhacker had thrown every cowboy who'd ridden him and only one rider had made it to the buzzer on Back Bender. "The odds aren't in your favor, McLean."

"Ladies and gentlemen." The rodeo announcer put an end to the cowboy banter. "As was broadcast earlier, due to one of our stock contractors encountering a flat tire, the rodeo committee has switched the order of events. Bull riding will take place next, followed by our final event of the day—the bareback competition."

The crowd booed its displeasure, but quieted when

the announcer continued his spiel. "You're about to witness some of the toughest and bravest men alive...."

Beau blocked out the booming voice and studied his draw—Gorgeous Gus. His new best friend was a veteran bull with a reputation for charging anything on two legs. Beau adjusted his protective vest and put on his face mask. He hated wearing the gear, but if he intended to win a title he'd sacrifice his vanity to remain healthy and injury-free. He climbed the chute rails and straddled the two-thousand-pound tiger-striped brindle Brahma-Hereford mix.

"Folks, I gotta say this next bull makes me nervous. Gorgeous Gus hails from the Henderson Ranch in Round Rock, Texas. Gus has already put three cowboys out of commission this season."

Music blared from the sound system but Beau kept his gaze averted from the JumboTron. He didn't care to watch as it replayed Jacob Montgomery's attempt to ride Gorgeous Gus in Denver this past July. Gus had thrown Montgomery and then, before the cowboy had gotten to his feet, the bull had gored his leg. A few seconds later the collective gasp that rippled through the stands sent chills down Beau's spine.

"Goin' head-to-horns with Gorgeous Gus is Beau Adams from Roundup, Montana. This is the first match-up between cowboy and bull."

Beau closed his eyes and envisioned Gus's exit out of the chute, but Sierra Byrne popped into his mind, interrupting his concentration.

"You ready, Adams?" the gateman asked.

"Not yet." Beau shook his head in an attempt to dislodge Sierra's blue eyes and flaming red hair from his memory. That he'd allowed the owner of the Number 1 Diner to mess with his focus didn't bode well for the next eight seconds. He flexed his fingers and worked the leather bull rope around his hand, fusing it to Gus's hide.

Breathe…in…out…in…out…. The blood pounded through his veins like roaring river rapids after the spring snowmelt in the Bull Mountains.

I'm the best.

No one can beat me.

Win.

He repeated the new mantra in his head—different from his previous pep talks when he'd taken a backseat to his brother's performances. Since Duke's retirement Beau had won several rodeos, but the bulls hadn't been rank bulls—not like the notorious Gorgeous Gus. A bead of sweat slid down Beau's temple. In a few seconds, he'd know if he'd been blowing hot air when he'd sparred with McLean. Satisfied with his grip, he crouched low and forced the muscles around the base of his spine to relax, then he signaled the gateman.

Gus exploded from the chute, twisting right as he kicked his back legs out. Beau survived the buck and Gus allowed him half a second to regain his balance before a series of kicks thrust Beau forward and he almost kissed the bull's horns. Beau ignored the burning fire spreading through his muscles as he squeezed his thighs against the animal's girth.

The dance went on…*twist, stomp, kick. Twist, stomp, kick.* Gus spun left then right in quick succession, almost ripping Beau's shoulder from its socket. Sheer determination and fear of being trampled kept him from flying off. The buzzer sounded and the bullfighters waved their hands in an attempt to catch Gus's attention.

Taking advantage of the distraction, Beau launched himself into the air. He hit the ground hard, the oxygen in his lungs bursting from his mouth like a six-pack belch. He didn't check on Gus—a one-second glance might mean the difference between making it to the rails...or not.

Ignoring the sharp twinge in his left ankle, Beau rolled to his feet and sprinted for safety. The mask on his helmet obscured the barrier, making it difficult to judge the distance. When his boot hit the bottom rung, a hand crossed his line of vision and a hard yank helped him over the top of the gate just as Gus rammed his head into the rails, the impact rattling the metal.

"Holy smokes! What a ride by Beau Adams!"

Applause thundered through the arena, and the ear-piercing racket of boots stomping on metal bleachers brought a smile to Beau's face as he removed his mask.

"Eighty-six is the score to beat!" The JumboTron replayed the bull ride.

"Congratulations, Beau."

Beau spun at the sound of the familiar voice. His cousin, Tuf Hart, stood a foot away, the corner of his mouth lifting in a cautious smile. "Tuf!" Beau clasped his cousin's hand and pulled him close for a chest bump and a stiff one-armed hug.

Tuf looked tired. Worn out. Maybe even a little beaten down. He'd left the Marines and returned to the States almost two years ago but had kept his distance from the family. Beau knew for a fact that his cousins Ace and Colt were upset with their baby brother for not returning to the ranch. Beau snagged Tuf's shirtsleeve and pulled him away from the chutes.

"Do you know how worried the family is about you?"

His cousin's gaze dropped to the tips of his boots.

"Fine. I won't pry. Just tell me you're okay."

"I'm getting there."

What the hell kind of answer was that? "Where've you been all this time?"

"I'd rather not say."

The youngest Hart had missed all the family weddings and good news. He bet Tuf hadn't heard that Ace and Flynn's first child was due around Thanksgiving or that Tuf's sister, Dinah, had married Austin Wright and they were expecting a baby next summer.

"Man, you gotta know your mom misses you."

Tuf removed his hat and shoved his fingers through his short brown hair. "I'll be in touch soon."

The twenty-eight-year-old standing before Beau was a stranger, not the cousin he remembered. "You don't know, do you?"

"Know what?"

"Aunt Sarah—"

"I can't talk right now." Tuf made a move to pass, but Beau blocked his path.

Didn't Tuf care that his mother had suffered an angina attack this past May and that the ranch had hit upon tough times? As a member of the family, Tuf should have known his mother had been forced to take Thunder Ranch in a new direction. Aunt Sarah had sold off most of the cattle, leased a sizable chunk of grazing land and had secured a hefty bank loan that Ace had cosigned.

"Call your mom and let her hear your voice."

The muscle along Tuf's jaw pulsed but he held his tongue.

Had something happened to his cousin in Afghanistan? The Tuf Beau had grown up with would never have shut out his family.

"Tell my mom I'm in Maryland and that I'm okay." His cousin walked off and joined the other bareback riders preparing for their event.

What was so important in Maryland that it prevented his cousin from returning to Thunder Ranch? Beau figured if Tuf had traveled this far west to compete in a rodeo he must be homesick. Hopefully, Tuf would come to his senses soon and haul his backside to Montana before Aunt Sarah dragged him home by his ear. Forgetting about his cousin, Beau focused on the Thunder Ranch bulls, eager to view their performances and he didn't want to miss Bushwhacker tossing McLean on his head.

"Next up is Pete Davis from Simpleton, North Dakota, riding Back Bender from the Thunder Ranch outside Roundup, Montana." The crowd applauded. "Back Bender's a young bull but he's got energy and lots of gas. This bull goes all-out for eight seconds and then some."

The announcer summed up Back Bender pretty well. The bull never ran out of kick—it was as if electricity flowed through the animal's veins instead of blood. When the gate opened, Back Bender erupted from the chute with a fierce kick before turning into a tight spin, then coming out of it with a double kick, which sent Davis flying at the three-second mark.

The bullfighters rushed in, but Back Bender continued to kick and the fans cheered in appreciation. Beau shook his head in wonder. The dang animal loved to buck.

"Like I said, folks, Back Bender's tough to ride and his brother, Bushwhacker is nastier. Turn your attention to chute number three for the final bull ride of the day."

Beau scaled the rails for a better view of the brown-and-red bull. Bushwhacker kicked the chute, warning those around him that he meant business.

"Bushwhacker also hails from Thunder Ranch and

this bull loves to ambush cowboys. He lulls a rider into thinking he'll make it to eight then tosses him into the dirt. Bushwhacker is undefeated this season. Let's see if Rusty McLean from Spokane, Washington, can outsmart this bull."

McLean adjusted the bull rope, his movements jerky and uneven. The boastful cowboy was nervous—he should be. He had a fifty-fifty chance of being the star of the day or going home the biggest loser.

C'mon, Bushwhacker. Show everyone why you're the best.

McLean signaled the gateman and Bushwhacker exploded into the arena. The bull's first buck was brutal—his signature move. He kicked both back legs out while twisting his hindquarters. Too bad for McLean. Bushwhacker's raw power unseated him, and the cowboy catapulted over the bull's head. McLean stumbled to his feet as the bullfighters intercepted Bushwhacker and escorted him from the arena. Staggering into the cowboy-ready area, McLean flung his bull rope and cussed.

"Better luck next time," Beau taunted.

The cowboy spit at the ground and stomped off.

"Beau Adams from Roundup, Montana, is the winner of today's bull-riding competition. Congratulations, Adams!"

Excited he'd taken first place, Beau collected his gear and the winning check, then found a seat in the stands to watch Tuf compete.

"Ladies and gentlemen, our final event of the day is the bareback competition. Those of you who don't know…a bareback horse is leaner, quicker and more agile than a saddle bronc. Bareback riding is rough, explosive, and the cowboys will tell ya that this event is the most physically demanding in rodeo." The crowd heckled the announcer, several fans shouting that bull riders were the toughest cowboys in the sport.

"Sit tight folks, you'll see what I'm talkin' about."

The announcer was right—a bareback cowboy's arm, neck and spine took a brutal beating and Beau worried about Tuf. If his cousin was just returning to competition, then he might not be in the best physical shape and the ride could end in disaster.

"First out of the gate is Tuf Hart, another cowboy from Roundup, Montana."

While Tuf settled onto the bronc and fiddled with his grip, the announcer continued. "Hart's gonna try to tame Cool Moon, a three-year-old gelding from the Circle T Ranch in New Mexico. Cool Moon is a spinner, folks."

Seconds later, the chute opened and Cool Moon went to work. The bronc twirled in tight, quick circles while bucking his back legs almost past vertical, the movement defying logic.

Hold on, Tuf. Hold on.

The moment Beau voiced the thought in his head, Tuf flew off Cool Moon. As soon as he hit the dirt, he got to his feet quickly. Beau watched him shuffle to the rails—no limp. His cousin hadn't won but more importantly he'd escaped injury.

After the final bareback rider competed, Beau made his way to the stock pens. Bushwhacker and Back Bender had rested for over an hour and it was time to load them into the trailer. First, he wanted to wish his cousin well and tell him to hurry home. He weaved through the maze of cowboys and rodeo fans, stopping once to autograph a program for a kid. Finally, he made it to the cowboy-ready area. "Hey, McLean," Beau called.

"Don't rub it in, Adams."

No need. Bushwhacker had had the final word. "Have you seen my cousin?"

"He left after his ride."

Miffed that Tuf hadn't cared enough to say goodbye, Beau sprinted to the parking lot then stopped. He didn't even know what vehicle Tuf drove. Disgusted, he retrieved the Thunder Ranch truck and livestock trailer.

With the help of two rodeo workers, Beau loaded Bushwhacker and Back Bender into the trailer. When he pulled out of the Sweetwater Events Complex, he drove north, intent on arriving home by the ten-thirty news. He made a pit stop for gas outside Rock Springs then purchased a large coffee and a Big Mac from the McDonald's restaurant inside the station. Back in his truck he popped three ibuprofen tablets to help with the swelling in his ankle—already his boot felt tight.

Once he merged onto the highway, he found a country-western station on the radio and settled in for the long drive. Less than five minutes passed before his thoughts turned to Sierra Byrne.

Physically, she was the opposite of the women he'd dated in the past. In heels, Sierra might reach five-seven. Full-figured—not slim or willowy—and red hair. He usually went for blondes.

Ah, but her eyes... Sierra's eyes had stopped Beau in his tracks the first time he'd gotten up the nerve to begin a conversation with her. Bright blue with a paler blue ring near the pupil. He'd locked gazes with her, mesmerized by the way the blue had brightened when she'd smiled.

And her hair... Sierra wore her hair in a springy

bob that ended an inch below her jaw, and her bangs
skimmed the corner of her right eye, lending her a playful, sexy look.

Her cuteness aside, there was something stirring…
vulnerable in Sierra's gaze that tugged at him. If only
he could get her to agree to a date with him. He'd first
asked her out this past June…then in July…then in
August…September. Each time she'd made up a lame
excuse about the diner keeping her too busy.

She was proving to be a challenge, but Beau wasn't
one to back down when the going got tough. Sierra
might have rebuffed his advances, but she wasn't as
clever at hiding her attraction to him. A few weeks ago,
she'd run into the edge of a table at the diner and he'd
rescued a plate of food from her hand. Their bodies had
collided, her lush breasts bumping his arm. Everyone
in the booth had heard her quiet gasp, but only Beau's
ears had caught the sexy purr that had followed.

Worrying about his love life wouldn't get him home
any faster. He switched the radio station to a sports talk
show and forgot about his crush on Sierra.

Five hours later, as Beau approached Roundup, he
noticed a vehicle parked on the side of the road. His
truck's headlights shone through the car's rear window,
illuminating a silhouette in the driver's seat. He turned
on the truck's flashers then pulled onto the shoulder
behind the car. When he approached the vehicle, the
driver's side window lowered several inches.

What the hell?

"Hello, Beau," Sierra said.

Well…well…well… This surely was his lucky day.

Chapter Two

Drat!

Sierra had the worst luck—go figure Beau Adams would end up rescuing her from her own stupidity.

Beau had set his sights on her early this spring when he'd begun eating at the diner on a regular basis. She found the handsome bull rider's attention flattering and would have jumped at the chance to date him, but circumstances beyond her control had forced her to keep him at arm's length.

"Engine trouble?" Beau's gaze drifted to her lips. The man had the most annoying habit of watching her mouth when they engaged in conversation.

"I'm not sure what the problem is," she said, ignoring her rising body temperature. There wasn't a thing wrong with her RAV4, except for the dent in the rear fender from a run-in with a minivan in the parking lot of the diner.

Sierra's sight had left her marooned on the side of the road.

He swept his hat from his head and ran his fingers through his hair. Beau's brown locks always looked in need of a trim, but it was his dark brown eyes and chiseled jaw that made her heart pound a little faster.

"I bet I can figure out what's wrong," he said.

Typical cowboy—believing he could repair anything and everything. Too bad Beau couldn't fix her eyes.

"How long have you been sitting here?"

Hours. "A short while." No way was she confessing that she couldn't see well enough to drive at night.

If not for a freeway wreck on the outskirts of Billings, she would have made it home, but ten miles from town dusk had turned to darkness. With few vehicles traveling the road, Sierra had decreased her speed and continued driving, but her confidence had been shattered when she'd crossed the center line and almost collided with another car. The near miss scared years off her life and she'd pulled onto the shoulder, resigned to wait until daybreak to drive into Roundup.

She'd phoned her aunt, who'd been visiting her since July, and had informed her that she planned to spend the night with a friend. Silence had followed Sierra's announcement. Everyone in town was aware of Beau's frequent visits to the diner and Jordan probably wondered if Sierra's *friend* happened to be Beau.

She appreciated that her aunt hadn't pried—after all, Sierra was thirty-one, old enough to have a sleepover with a man. In truth, she'd love to get to know Beau better, but life wasn't fair. Too bad he'd happened along tonight. She'd been certain she'd get out of this mess without anyone the wiser.

"Pop the hood," he said.

"There's no need. I called Davidson Towing. Stan is out on another call but should be here in a little while." Maybe if she distracted Beau, he'd forget about checking the engine. "Returning from a rodeo?"

"Yep. Hauled a couple of Thunder Ranch bulls down to Rock Springs, Wyoming."

"Did you compete?"

He rested an arm along the top of the car. "Sure did, and I won." His cocky grin warmed her better than her down parka.

"Congratulations." The diner's patrons kept Sierra up to date on their hometown cowboys' accomplishments. Since she'd moved to Roundup five years ago, most of the gossip about the Adams twins focused on Duke's rodeo successes. Lately, Beau was getting his turn in the spotlight.

"Wanna see my buckle?"

She swallowed a laugh. "Sure." He removed the piece of silver from his coat pocket and passed it through the open window. "It's beautiful."

"There's no need for you to freeze. Stan'll tow your car to his garage and square the bill with you in the morning." Beau reached for the door handle.

"No!" Sierra cringed. She hadn't meant to shout. For a girl who'd lived most of her life in Chicago, small towns were both a blessing and a curse. She handed Beau the buckle. "I appreciate the offer, but I'd prefer to wait with my car."

Instead of backing away he poked his head through the window, his hair brushing the side of her face. A whiff of faded cologne—sandalwood and musk—swirled beneath her nose. "Just checking to make sure there's no serial killer in the backseat holding you hostage."

Oh, brother.

"If you're determined to wait for Stan, then sit in my truck. I've got the heat going and I'll share the coffee I bought at the rest stop."

"Thanks, but you should get your bulls back to the ranch." *C'mon, Beau. Give up and go home.*

"I don't like the idea of you waiting out here all alone."

"This is Roundup, Montana. Nothing's going to happen to me."

"You're forgetting the break-ins this past summer. This area is no Mayberry, U.S.A."

Sierra regretted her flippant remark. Although Roundup had been and would continue to be a safe place to live and raise a family, a rash of thefts in the ranching community had put people on edge for a while. Even Beau had been victimized when one of his custom-made saddles had been stolen and sold at a truck stop miles away.

"I'll be fine. Besides, your cousin caught those thieves." She switched on the interior light and pointed to her winter coat. "And I'm plenty warm." A flat tire during her first winter in Big Sky country had taught Sierra to keep a heavy jacket in her vehicle year-round. Unlike Chicago, car trouble in rural Montana could mean waiting an entire day for help to arrive and the state's weather was anything but predictable—sixty degrees one hour, a blizzard the next.

"How long did you say you've been waiting for Stan?"

"Twenty minutes maybe." When had she become such an accomplished liar?

Beau walked to the front of the car and placed his hand on the hood.

Busted. She'd been parked for over three hours—surely the engine was stone cold. "Thanks again for stopping to check on me," she called out the window, hoping he'd take the hint and leave.

"You're sure you don't want a ride to the diner?"

"Positive."

"Okay. Take care." He retreated to his truck where he took his dang tootin' time pulling back onto the road.

As soon as the livestock trailer disappeared around the bend in the road, Sierra breathed a sigh of relief.

Then the tears fell.

Ah, Beau. Darn the man for being…nice. Handsome. Sexy.

Over a year ago, Sierra had become aware of the subtle changes in her eyesight, but she'd steadfastly ignored the signs and had gone about life as usual. Her resolve to pretend her vision was fine had grown stronger after each encounter with Beau. Then her aunt had arrived unannounced—thanks to the busybodies who'd informed her of Sierra's recent mishaps around town—determined to persuade Sierra to schedule an appointment with an ophthalmologist. Sadly, she didn't need an examination to tell her that she'd inherited the gene for the eye disease that had led to her aunt's blindness.

Why couldn't Beau have paid attention to her when she'd first arrived in Roundup years ago? Darn life for being unfair. Sierra rested her head on the back of the seat. Maybe she'd see—*ha, ha, ha*—things in a different light come morning.

Morning arrived at 6:25 a.m., when a semi truck whizzed by her car and woke her. She wiggled her cold toes and fingers until the feeling returned to the numb digits. If she hurried, she'd have time to mix a batch of biscuits before the diner doors opened for breakfast at seven.

She snapped on her seat belt then checked the rearview mirror. *Oh. My. God.* Beau's pickup, minus the livestock trailer, sat a hundred yards behind her. Embarrassed and humiliated that he'd caught her red-handed in a lie, she shoved the key into the ignition and the SUV engine fired to life. After checking for cars in both directions she hit the gas. The back tires spewed gravel as she pulled onto the highway. Keeping a death grip on the steering wheel she glanced at the side mirror—Beau remained fast asleep, slouched against the driver's-side window.

Don't you dare cry.

Her eyesight was blurry in the mornings, and if she gave into the tears that threatened to fall she'd be forced to pull off the road again—and then what excuse would she give Beau?

BEAU WOKE IN time to catch the taillights of Sierra's SUV driving off. The least she could have done was thank him for watching over her through the night.

Sierra mystified him. After finding her stranded on the side of the road he'd been puzzled by her insistence that he not wait with her for a tow. Then, when he'd placed his hand on the hood of the car and discovered the engine was cold, his suspicions had grown. For the life of him he couldn't figure out what she'd been up to, but she'd made it clear she didn't want his help, so he'd moseyed along. When he'd reached Roundup, he'd driven past Davidson Towing. Stan's tow truck had sat parked in the lot, the lights turned off in the service garage.

For a split second, Beau had wondered if Sierra had intended to rendezvous with a man, but he'd nixed that idea. Before he'd begun his campaign to convince her to go out on a date with him he'd asked his cousin Dinah, the town's sheriff, to find out if Sierra was involved with another man. According to Dinah's sources Sierra wasn't. Boyfriend or not, Beau hadn't been about to leave Sierra alone in the dark.

He'd delivered Bushwhacker and Back Bender to Thunder Ranch, then had hollered at his father through the door that he was meeting up with friends at the Open Range Saloon. Alibi taken care of, he'd hightailed it back to the highway.

When he'd passed her SUV, the truck's headlights had shown her asleep in the front seat. Alone. Relieved he'd been wrong about a clandestine meeting, he'd parked behind the car, resigned to wait until morning for answers. Those answers were right now fleeing down the highway.

Although tempted to stalk Sierra until she offered an explanation for the crazy stunt she'd pulled last night, he started his truck and turned onto the county road that bypassed Roundup and brought him to the back side of Thunder Ranch, where the Adams men were in charge of the bucking bulls and the cattle that grazed this section of the property. He pulled up to the small house his father had raised him and his brother in after their mother had died in a car accident thirty years ago. He shut off the engine then tapped a finger against the steering wheel. Was he coming on too strong with Sierra?

When he'd first begun pursuing her, his brother had pointed out that folks might mistake his actions as those of a man on the rebound. He'd discarded Duke's words. Beau and his former girlfriend Melanie had given their long-distance relationship a shot but they'd grown apart months before their official breakup last December. Now that Duke and all their cousins, except Tuf, had married, Beau was feeling left out of the holy-matrimony club. He wanted for himself the same happiness his brother and cousins had found with their significant others, and something about Sierra made Beau believe she could be the one.

He hopped out of the truck and used the side door

to enter the house. He found his father sitting at the kitchen table, eating donuts—usually by this time in the morning he was checking the water tanks and feed bins in the bull pasture. Beau hung his sheepskin jacket on the hook by the door. "Skipping your oatmeal and English muffin today?"

"Jordan sent the donuts home with me last night. Leftovers from the diner."

Jordan Peterson was Sierra's aunt and his father's… friend…girlfriend? The moment Jordan had stepped off the bus with her seeing-eye dog in July, his father had been hot on her heels. Beau had no idea where the older couple's relationship was headed, but he was ticked off that his father spent most of his time with Jordan and neglected his responsibilities around the ranch.

"When did you get in last night?" Had his father been home when Beau had dropped off the bulls?

"'Round midnight."

Guess not.

"Since we're keeping tabs on each other's where-abouts…." His father nodded at Beau's jacket. "Where'd you hang your hat last night?"

Admitting that he'd slept in the cab of his truck would raise more questions than Beau cared to answer. Besides, he doubted Sierra wanted her aunt or the good folks of Roundup to learn she'd spent the night on the side of the road.

Rather than lie, Beau changed the subject. "Did you eat supper at the Number 1 yesterday?"

"Only an emergency would keep me from missing the Saturday special."

Beef potpie baked in a homemade crust. Beau had memorized the daily specials when he'd begun his campaign to woo Sierra.

His father carried his coffee cup to the sink. "Sierra phoned Jordan and said she wouldn't be back in town until morning, so I helped close up the diner last night."

Sierra had covered all her bases—clever girl—but why?

"Speaking of Sierra…Jordan tells me that you've been dropping by the diner every day."

Beau never talked about his personal life with his father and didn't feel comfortable now. "Do you have a problem with that?"

"As a matter of fact, I do. I want you to keep away from Sierra."

Beau's hackles rose. He and his father had never been close, and up until now his dad had kept his nose out of Beau's affairs. Why all of a sudden did he care if Beau had his sights set on Sierra? "I'm a grown man. I don't need your permission to date a woman."

"You don't have time for a relationship right now."

"And you do?" Beau asked.

"What's that supposed to mean?"

"You and Jordan are becoming awfully tight." Beau and his father exchanged glowers.

"Instead of chasing after Sierra, you should focus on mending fences with your brother. There's a lot of work around here and if you're squabbling with each other things don't get done."

Afraid he'd say something he shouldn't, Beau helped himself to the last donut on the plate and poured a cup of coffee.

"You talk to your brother lately?" his father asked.

"No. Why?"

"Duke said you've been giving him the cold shoulder since he quit rodeo."

Not exactly true. Beau was still talking to Duke—he

just didn't go out of his way to do so. After their blow-up this past summer, he'd had a few superficial conversations with his brother, but they'd steered clear of discussing rodeo. Beau accepted most of the blame for having kept his distance from Duke—he needed time to come to grips with all the changes in his brother's life.

"You hurt Duke's pride when you told him you'd never given your best effort in the arena all these years."

Where did his father get off lecturing Beau? If the old man had shown a scrap of concern or compassion over Duke's childhood stuttering, or defended Duke from bullies, Beau wouldn't have felt compelled to do the job, which had naturally led Beau to allowing Duke the limelight to build his self-esteem.

"I never told you that you had to be second best," his father said.

"No, but you were oblivious to Duke's struggles. Someone had to encourage him."

"I wasn't oblivious." His father's gaze shifted to the wall. "Figured if I ignored his stuttering, Duke would grow out of it faster."

Part of Beau felt sorry for his father—raising twin boys without a wife would be a challenge for any man. Even so, had his father shown any compassion for Duke, Beau might not have overstepped his bounds with his brother.

"The only reason you want me to make nice with Duke is because you've been shirking your duties around here and you need your sons to pick up the slack."

His father's steely-eyed glare warned Beau he was treading on thin ice—time to change the subject. "A while back Duke said you were thinking about retiring." He hoped the news wasn't true.

"Been tossing around the idea."

The timing couldn't be worse—Beau adding rodeos to his schedule and Duke trying to balance family and his job as deputy sheriff. Then again, his father only considered what was best for him—never mind the rest of the family. "Why retire?"

"What do you mean, why? That's what men do when they get old—they quit working."

Joshua Adams was fifty-eight years old and although ranching took a toll on a man's body, his father didn't look or act as if he was ready to spend the rest of his life twiddling his thumbs.

"Does this urge for less work and more free time have anything to do with Earl McKinley leasing his land and moving to Billings?" Joshua Adams had punched cows for Earl's father until Beau's mother had died, then Aunt Sarah had talked her brother into moving closer to family and working for her husband at Thunder Ranch.

"I don't care what Earl does," his father said.

"Ever since Jordan arrived in town you haven't cared about anything but spending time with her."

"You got a problem with that?"

Maybe. "Aunt Sarah isn't sure if she's going to keep Midnight. If she sells the stallion then we may have to invest more in our bucking bulls and Asteroid needs a lot of attention." Beau didn't have time to deal with the young bull, but his father did.

"Midnight and Asteroid will be fine. You worry too much."

And the old man didn't worry enough.

"Whatever you decide about retirement, I hope you put it off another year."

"Why's that?"

"I'm making a run at an NFR title next year. I'll be on the road a lot."

"You think you can win that many rodeos?"

"I don't think—I know I can."

A horn blast sent Beau to the back door. "It's Colt." His cousin's truck and horse trailer barreled up the drive. "Aunt Sarah's with him." Beau snatched his jacket from the hook and his father followed him outside.

"It's Midnight," Colt said as he rounded the hood of his Dodge.

The newest addition to the bucking-stock operation, The Midnight Express, was wreaking havoc at Thunder Ranch.

"Something the matter with Midnight, Sarah?" Beau's father asked.

"He's run off again. Gracie thinks one of her boys accidently left the latch on the stall door unhooked when they were helping her in the barn this morning." Gracie was Midnight's primary caretaker and no doubt in a state of panic over the valuable horse.

This past summer, Midnight had suffered a flesh wound from a run-in with barbed wire after he'd escaped his stall and had gone missing for over a month. Although the horse was fully healed, Ace had kept Midnight's physical activity to a minimum, which didn't include a ten-mile sprint across the ranch.

Beau's father put his arm around his sister's shoulder. "Don't get yourself worked up. The stress isn't good for your heart."

"What about the paddocks?" Beau asked. "Maybe Midnight jumped a fence to get to one of the mares."

"We checked. He's running free somewhere on the property," Colt said.

Beau shielded his eyes against the bright sunlight and searched the horizon.

"Help Colt look for Midnight, Beau. He can't have gone far." Joshua motioned toward the house. "There's hot coffee in the kitchen, Sarah. I'll be in after I check on the bulls."

Once his father was out of earshot, Beau asked, "Does Ace know Midnight's on the run?"

"Not yet. I was hoping to put the horse back in his stall before my brother got wind of it," Colt said.

"We'll find him."

"You head north on the four-wheeler and I'll meet you there with the trailer." Colt handed Beau a walkie-talkie then hopped into his truck and took off.

Before Beau forgot, he fished his wallet from his back pocket and removed the cashier's check for three thousand dollars. "I won yesterday." He held the draft out to his aunt.

She didn't take the money. "Congratulations."

"C'mon, Aunt Sarah." He waved the check. "It'll help pay for some of the expense that went into searching for Midnight over the summer."

The Midnight Express had cost Thunder Ranch a hefty $38,000, and when the stallion had gone AWOL the family had shelled out big bucks—money they could ill afford in this bad economy—to locate the horse. In the end, the dang stallion had been right under their noses at Buddy Wright's neighboring ranch.

Reluctantly his aunt accepted the check. "Thank you, Beau." She sighed. "I'm worried I made a mistake in believing Midnight could bring Thunder Ranch back from the brink."

"Midnight's not just any horse, Aunt Sarah. He'll come through for us." Midnight's pedigree had been traced back to the infamous bucking horse, Five Minutes to Midnight, who lay buried at the National Cowboy Hall of Fame. If given half a chance, Beau believed the stallion could win another NFR title.

Beau opened his mouth to tell his aunt he'd run into Tuf at the rodeo but changed his mind. She was already upset over Midnight; mentioning Tuf might cause her heart to act up. "Keep the coffee hot, Aunt Sarah." Beau kissed her cheek then jogged to the equipment shed where the ATVs were stored.

A minute later, he took off, the cold wind whipping his face as he wove through two miles of pine trees. When he cleared the forest, he spotted Midnight drinking at the stock pond. Beau stopped the four-wheeler and pulled out the walkie-talkie. "Midnight's at the pond."

"Be right there."

The ATV's rumbling engine caught Midnight's attention. The coal-black stallion pawed the ground. In that moment, Beau felt he and Midnight were kindred spirits—both needed to prove they were the best, yet neither had competed in enough rodeos this season to make it to Vegas and show the world they were number one.

Colt arrived, leaving the truck parked several yards away. He grabbed a rope and joined Beau. "Is he spooked?"

"Nope." Midnight was the cockiest horse Beau had ever been around.

"Since he came back from Buddy's he's been more difficult to handle," Colt said.

"I've got an opinion, if you care to hear it."

"Speak your mind."

"Midnight's jaunt across the ranch is his way of letting us know he's feeling penned in and he's ready for a challenge."

"By challenge, you mean rodeo."

"Midnight's a competitor. Bucking's in his blood. He's not happy unless he's throwing cowboys off his back."

"You might be right. He's probably feeling restless now that Fancy Gal's expecting and wants nothing to do with him."

No wonder the stallion was acting out of sorts—his companion mare was snubbing her nose at him. "Enter Midnight in the Badlands Bull Bash." The one-day event had a purse of fifty thousand dollars.

"Ace would have my head if I took that horse anywhere without telling him," Colt said. "A win, though, will increase Midnight's stud fees."

"Sure would."

"I'll talk to Ace." Colt pointed to the stallion. "You ready?"

"Nothing I like better than a good chase."

"Keep him penned in until I get close enough to throw a rope over his head."

Midnight allowed Colt to get within fifty feet of him, then when Colt raised his roping arm, the stallion took off. Beau followed on the ATV, cutting Midnight off at the pass. The horse spun, then galloped in the opposite direction. Beau turned Midnight back toward Colt. The game went on for several minutes. Finally, Midnight exhausted himself and Colt threw the rope over the horse's head.

"Nice work," Colt said after Beau shut off the four-wheeler.

"Midnight could have escaped if he'd wanted to."

"Yeah, I know." Colt tugged on the rope and led the

stallion to the truck, Midnight snorting hot steam into the brisk air.

Beau followed the pair and opened the trailer doors, then lowered the ramp. Midnight tossed his head and reared. Colt gave him plenty of rope, then waved his hand in front of the stallion's nose. Midnight clomped up the ramp and into the trailer.

"Why are you the only one who can get that horse to load?"

Colt opened his fist to reveal a peppermint candy. "Don't tell Ace my secret." Midnight poked his head out the trailer window, and Colt gave the stallion his reward then latched the door. "Thanks for your help, Beau. I promised Leah we'd take the kids to an early-bird matinee. Now we won't be late."

Colt had seamlessly adjusted to married life and fatherhood, but Beau was curious. "When's the family going to meet your son?" His cousin had confessed to the family that he'd fathered a child twelve years ago but had only recently made contact with the boy. Colt was also stepdad to Leah's son and daughter.

"I'm not sure. I invited Evan to spend Thanksgiving at the ranch but I'm leaving it up to him to decide when he's ready to meet the family."

Speaking of family... "Hey, Colt."

"Yeah?"

"I ran into Tuf in Rock Springs."

"You didn't tell my mom, did you?"

"No. I thought you and Ace should be the ones to tell her if you think she should know. I was worried the news might upset her."

"Is he okay?"

"Hard to say. I asked when he was coming home, but he didn't know."

Colt stubbed the ground with the toe of his boot.

"I suggested he call your mom, but—" Beau shrugged.

"I'm not one to judge. I didn't always uphold my share of responsibility around the ranch through the years, but I kept in touch with my mother. The least Tuf can do is call home once in a while." Colt hopped into the front seat of the truck. "Thanks again for your help."

"Sure thing. Enjoy the movies."

After Colt departed, Beau stood in the cold, staring into the distance. Today was Sunday and he had a hankering for beef sirloin tip roast—Sunday special at the Number 1. He'd return to the house and help his father with ranch chores, then shower and head into town to do some more chasing…of the two-legged variety.

Chapter Three

Sierra climbed the steps of the hidden staircase inside the diner's pantry and entered her living room. There were only two ways into the upstairs apartment—the staircase and the fire escape behind the building.

"It's me, Aunt Jordan. I brought you a late lunch—baked potato soup and a roll." She set the food on the kitchen table.

Her aunt's seeing-eye dog, Molly, ventured from the guest bedroom first, followed by her owner. Sierra was amazed at how quickly Jordan had learned the layout of the apartment and could navigate the space without bumping into any furniture.

"Have you been a good girl, Molly?" Sierra scratched the yellow lab behind the ears. Jordan washed her hands at the sink then sat at the table and confidently familiarized herself with the items before her—take-out soup container, wheat roll inside a paper towel, butter dish, knife and spoon.

"This was nice of you, dear." Her aunt buttered the roll. "What time did you get in this morning? I didn't hear you."

"Early." Sierra disliked being evasive but she'd been on pins and needles, worried Beau would drop by the diner and demand an explanation for her bizarre behavior last night. She owed him the truth, but facing reality took more courage than she possessed at the moment.

Hoping to dissuade her aunt from prying into her whereabouts, Sierra asked, "What did you do last night?" Several of Jordan's friends from high school lived in the area and often invited her out to eat or shop.

"Joshua helped Irene close the diner, then we watched a movie up here."

"Watched…?" Her aunt possessed a wicked sense of humor regarding her blindness, but Sierra didn't see a darn thing funny about having to live in the dark.

"Joshua watched. I listened."

Since returning to Montana, Jordan had been spending a lot of time with her old boyfriend, which Sierra couldn't be more pleased about. She'd love for her aunt to sell her condo in Florida and relocate to Roundup.

"This tastes similar to your mother's recipe, but there's something different…"

"Rosemary. I used it a lot in cooking school." Sierra poured two glasses of iced tea and joined her aunt at the table.

"Your mother was so proud when you graduated from that famous Cordon Bleu program," Aunt Jordan said.

"Mom always envied your talent for dancing."

Jordan reached across the table and Sierra clasped her hand. "I wish your mother were still with us."

"Me, too." Sierra's parents had died in a plane crash five years ago. A former Air Force pilot and captain for United Airlines, her father had survived near misses and engine malfunctions, yet it had been a summer thunderstorm that had brought down her parents' twin-engine Cessna while flying to their cabin along Musselshell River.

"Do you have any regrets, moving from Chicago to Roundup?" Jordan asked.

"None." After her parents' funeral, Sierra had decided to use her inheritance to renovate the old newspaper building in town and turn it into a diner where she could put her catering recipes to good use.

"Your mother would have loved helping you run the diner."

Sierra was sad that she hadn't been able to share her business venture with her parents, but at least they'd been spared the agony of watching their only child face monumental, life-altering changes. Then again, Sierra would have appreciated their support when the going got tough…tougher…toughest. At least her aunt was by her side, and Sierra hoped she would remain so for a long time to come.

"Don't feel you have to keep me company," Jordan said. "I imagine it's busy downstairs."

"Irene has everything under control." Sierra's second in command ran the diner like a military mess hall. Even the two high school students Sierra employed toed the line when they worked with Irene. "Mind if I ask you a personal question, Aunt Jordan?"

"Not at all." Her aunt's smile erased ten years from her age.

"How serious were you and Joshua when you dated in high school?"

A wistful expression settled over her aunt's face. "We were very much in love."

"What happened?"

"I wanted to go to college and see the world, and Joshua was content to remain in Roundup."

"Mom said she never regretted leaving town, but I think that's because she and Dad spent their summers at the cabin. Do you wish you would have stayed closer to home?"

"No. I needed to spread my wings. I knew if I wanted a dancing career that I'd have to move to California."

"Then you met Uncle Bob in Sacramento."

"And Bob showed me the world through the military."

Did her aunt realized how fortunate she'd been to be able to *see* all her dreams come true before her eye disease had caused her to go blind?

You've seen your dreams come true.

She'd become a chef and had opened her own business, honoring her great-grandfather who'd died in a flood at the Number 1 Mine outside Roundup. But what about her wanting to marry and have children? The odds of that wish coming true were a long shot.

"What happened to your dance career after you married Uncle Bob?"

"I cut back on my performances, then eventually quit when we decided to have children. I knew I'd have to put on weight before I became pregnant." She paused. "In the end, my weight didn't matter. I couldn't get pregnant."

"I'm sorry, Aunt Jordan."

"I had just talked your uncle into agreeing to try in vitro fertilization when I noticed something wasn't right with my eyes."

"How old were you?" Sierra asked.

"Thirty-three." Jordan sighed. "After the doctor confirmed that I'd eventually go blind, Bob insisted we stop trying to have children." Her aunt waved a hand before her face. "Life goes on. Speaking of which, you need to make an appointment with an ophthalmologist."

"I've got time." Sierra wasn't ready for an official diagnosis.

"Sandra—" Aunt Jordan's high school friend "—was in the diner last week and said you walked right by her without saying hello."

Since Jordan helped in the diner once in a while, the place had become a coffee klatch for her gossipy friends. "I wasn't rude on purpose."

"I didn't think you were."

"I'm sure I was distracted." Sierra would rather believe that than admit she had trouble with her peripheral vision.

"You don't have to be afraid."

"I'm not afraid." Sierra was scared—bone-chillingly terrified of going blind. "Are you sure you won't miss spending the holidays with your friends in St. Petersburg?" Her aunt had rented her condo to a businessman until the end of the year.

"Is that a polite way of telling me I'm cramping your style?"

"Not at all." It was Sierra's way of conveying that she didn't want her aunt to leave Roundup. *Ever.* Jordan had leaned on her husband as her eyesight had worsened through the years, but Sierra had no one to guide her down the frightening road ahead. "It's just that Montana winters are long and cold."

"I remember them, dear. I'm looking forward to snow for the holidays."

"I'm sure it will be nice to spend Christmas with Joshua." If her aunt and former boyfriend really hit it off, Jordan would have another reason to remain in Roundup.

"Thank you for reminding me that I need to make a Christmas list. I have no idea what Joshua would like."

Sierra took her glass to the sink. "I'm sure he'll be pleased with whatever you choose for him." It was obvious that Joshua was crazy for Jordan—not a day went by that he didn't visit her or call.

"I think I'll read this afternoon," Jordan said.

As much as Sierra loved her aunt and needed her encouragement, there were times when she grew weary of being impressed by the woman. Jordan had taught herself to read braille before she'd completely lost her eyesight. "Would Molly like a walk before I leave?"

"I'm sure she would, but she'll have to wait until three."

"I forgot about her schedule." Molly was on a set timetable for eating, walks and bedtime. "Holler if you need anything, Aunt Jordan."

"I won't, dear."

That was the truth. No one had been more surprised than Sierra when her aunt and Molly had ridden a Greyhound bus clear across the country by themselves. From the very first day in town, her aunt had demonstrated her independence. It didn't take long to learn Jordan became perturbed when people did things for her without asking if she needed their help. Sierra was counting on her aunt to teach her how to be just as gutsy and courageous.

Sierra took the back stairs down to the diner. Sunday was her favorite day of the week. Roundup's spiritual citizens attended morning church services at the various places of worship, and afterward many of them stopped by the diner for lunch. Folks were usually in a congenial mood after listening to God's word, and her employees swore tips were better on Sundays than any other day of the week.

When Sierra entered the kitchen she found her

waitresses sharing a piece of peach cobbler. "Taking a break?"

"Yeah. Mr. Humphrey finally left," Amy said. "The old fart drives me crazy." The teen snorted. "Who leaves a tip in nickels?"

That her waitress found Mr. Humphrey an odd duck amused Sierra. Amy possessed her share of interesting traits, such as short, dark hair with hot-pink bangs. Tattoos covered Amy's right arm from wrist to shoulder, and she wore numerous silver rings in her ears and fake diamond studs pierced her nose and eyebrows.

"Mr. Humphrey is one of my faithful customers. Please be nice to him," Sierra said.

"I always am," Amy grumbled.

Amy was a nice girl, but she ran with a rough crowd and had gotten caught shoplifting twice this year. Dinah Hart-Wright, Roundup's sheriff, had asked Sierra if she'd give Amy a job to help keep her out of trouble. The teen's first few weeks at the diner had been a challenge, but Susie, an honor student at the high school and one year younger than Amy, had befriended the delinquent teen and shown her the ropes.

"When you girls finish your dessert, please clean off the mustard and ketchup bottles, then fill the salt and pepper shakers on the tables."

"Sure. But Sierra," Susie said. "I checked the storeroom this morning and we're out of salt."

"Okay, thanks for letting me know." Sierra had taken inventory a week ago and hadn't noticed they were low on salt. Had it been an oversight on her part or had she not *seen* that the salt canister had been missing from the shelf?

"Did you enjoy your visit with your friend?" Irene asked when Sierra joined her behind the lunch counter.

"What frien—" Sierra caught herself. "Um, yes. Thanks for closing up last night. I'm sorry it was such short notice."

Irene waved her off. "We all need a little downtime. Speaking of which, Karla agreed to work the rest of my shift this afternoon."

"Aren't you feeling well?" Because Irene's husband was a long-haul truck driver, she often worked more than an eight-hour day so she didn't have to sit at home alone. Maybe the long hours were catching up with the fifty-year-old.

"Ed called. His run to Boise got canceled. He's coming home tonight."

"That's great news. Be sure to fix a plate of food for each of you before clocking out."

"Thanks, Sierra. The less time I spend in the kitchen the more time Ed and I can spend in the bedroom." Irene winked. "I'll finish getting the potatoes ready and put the pans of sirloin into the oven before I leave." Irene returned to the kitchen, leaving Sierra alone in the diner.

The rumble of a truck engine caught her attention and she glanced out the front window. Beau's red Dodge pulled into a parking spot across the street in front of Wright's Western Wear and Tack. He got out of the truck and glanced over his shoulder. Sierra ducked behind the counter, hoping he hadn't caught her spying. After counting to five, she stood. Beau strolled along the sidewalk, his cocky swagger tugging a quiet sigh from her. She loved the way he filled out his Wranglers.

Go talk to him.

She owed Beau an apology and a plausible explanation for why she'd spent the night in her car—as soon as she got up the courage.

"HEY, AUSTIN," BEAU called out a greeting when he entered Wright's. He'd driven into town to speak with Sierra but at the last minute had decided to check on his saddles.

"Heard you took first place in the bull-riding competition yesterday." Boot heels clunked against the wood floor as Austin wove through the racks of clothing.

Beau shook hands with his cousin's husband. "Word gets around quick in this town." How long would it take for people to gossip about him and Sierra if he persuaded her to go on a date with him?

"Colt phoned Dinah a while ago. Good thing you two caught Midnight before he escaped the boundaries of the ranch." Austin shook his head. "My wife doesn't need the aggravation of working a second missing-horse case on that stallion."

"Is Dinah's pregnancy making her moody?"

"No comment." Austin grinned. "Hey, before I forget." He reached into his shirt pocket and removed a business card. "This guy's interested in having you make him a saddle."

"He didn't like either of those?" Beau glanced at the saddles in the front window.

"He wants a cutting saddle with a shallower seat and a higher horn." Austin motioned to the business card in Beau's hand. "Jim Phillips is the new foreman at the Casey Beef Ranch south of Billings."

"Did you give Phillips one of my cards?" Beau asked.

"Sure did. He said he'd call in a few days."

Beau shoved Phillips's contact information into the back pocket of his jeans. "How's married life?" Heavy footfalls sounded overhead and both men looked up at the decorative tin ceiling.

"Married life is good. Real good."

The bell on the door clanged and Ace Hart entered the store, wearing a scowl. Beau attempted to humor his cousin. "For a man who's about to become a father, you don't look too happy." When the teasing remark failed to lighten Ace's somber expression, Beau said, "Flynn's feeling okay, isn't she?"

"Aside from swollen ankles she's fine, thanks for asking."

"What's the matter? You look pissed," Austin said.

Ace stared pointedly at Beau. "Colt said you suggested Midnight compete in South Dakota next month."

"A win there would increase his breeding value," Beau said.

"I know better than anyone when Midnight's fit to compete again." Ace rubbed his brow.

Beau sympathized with the tough position his older cousin was in. Ace was under a lot of pressure to insure the family's investment paid off. If the stallion got injured, had to be put down, or for some reason could not be bred, Ace could lose his livelihood. With a baby on the way, his cousin had to protect his interests.

"Are you saying Midnight can't compete next month?" Beau asked.

"I haven't made up my mind," Ace said. "By the way, congrats on your win."

Austin slapped Beau on the back. "You sure are lighting up the circuit since Duke quit."

"Mind if I have a minute alone with Beau?" Ace asked.

"No problem. I'll be in the storeroom."

After Austin walked out of earshot, Ace spoke. "Colt mentioned you ran into Tuf in Wyoming." The lines bracketing Ace's mouth deepened. "Did he seem okay?"

"He said he's working through some stuff."

"Tuf needs to come home."

For as long as Beau remembered, Ace had been the strong, confident one in the family. At times his cousin could be too rigid, too controlling, but there was no hiding the concern in the man's eyes for his little brother. Ace cared deeply about his family and wanted Tuf home where he could be looked after.

The bell on the door clanged a second time. *Sierra.*

"Let me know if you run into Tuf again."

"I will."

Ace left, tipping his hat to Sierra on the way out.

Once the door shut behind Beau's cousin, Sierra's smile wilted.

"I was planning to stop by the diner after I talked with Austin," Beau said, closing the gap between them.

"I'm sorry, I didn't mean to interrupt." She grappled for the door handle.

"Wait." Beau pried Sierra's fingers from the knob but didn't release her hand. "I finished my business with Austin. Walk with me?"

"Sure."

He ushered Sierra outside then led her around the corner. Single-story homes lined the street and a small park sat in the middle of the block. "If you're cold we can talk in the diner," he said. The afternoon temperature was in the low forties, but there wasn't a cloud in the sky.

"I'm fine. The sun feels good on my face."

They strolled in silence, Beau holding Sierra's hand. That she didn't pull away stroked his ego. When they reached the park, he guided her to the lone bench near the swing set. "You don't have to worry," he said. "I won't pressure you for an explanation about last night."

"That's generous, but…" She twirled a button on her

coat then noticed her action and shoved her hand into a pocket. "How do you feel about your dad and my aunt dating?" she asked.

Amused by the delay tactic, he chuckled. Heck, no one was more surprised than Beau that his father was goo-goo eyes over Jordan Peterson.

"I'm serious, Beau. Are you okay with their relationship? Because I believe my aunt really cares for your father."

He'd be a lot happier about the matchup if Jordan didn't distract his father from his ranch chores, but Beau didn't want to discuss the older couple. "They're both adults. They don't need anyone's permission to date." He opened his mouth to change the subject when a shout down the block drew his attention.

"Z-Zorro!" Duke's stepson, Luke, chased Duke's German shepherd. The dog sprinted, the leash flying in the air behind him. The seven-year-old was no match for Zorro and Beau made a dash for the sidewalk.

"Zorro, heel!" Beau extended his arm and the dog skidded to a stop, his legs becoming entangled with his leash. Luke caught up, his little chest heaving.

"Th-thanks, Uncle Beau." Luke took the leash. "B-bad dog, Zorro."

"Where's your mom?" Normally Angie didn't let her son out of her sight.

"T-talking with Dad in the jail. I was t-taking Zorro for a w-walk but—" Luke sucked in several breaths.

Pitying the kid's miniature lungs Beau said, "Come with me. There's someone who'd like to meet Zorro." Beau steered Luke and the dog toward the park bench.

"Hi, Luke," Sierra said. "I guess Zorro wanted a run, not a walk."

Luke smiled. "He went after M-Molly."

Sierra spoke to Beau. "My aunt takes her seeing-eye dog for a stroll around town in the afternoons." She switched her attention to Luke. "Is Molly still with my aunt?"

"Yeah. M-Molly never runs off."

Sierra rubbed Zorro's head. "Poor boy…chasing after a lady who doesn't want you."

Beau cringed. He hoped Sierra's comment hadn't been meant for him.

"Luke! Luke, where are you?"

"Here!" Beau waved at his brother and Duke jogged toward the group.

"What happened?" Duke asked.

"Z-Zorro s-saw—"

"Slow down." Duke laid a hand on the boy's shoulder.

"Zorro saw Molly and ran away." Duke had a calming effect on his stepson and Luke stopped stuttering.

"Good thing Uncle Beau was here." Duke glanced at Sierra and switched the subject. "Did you have car trouble yesterday?"

Face flushing Sierra mumbled, "Ahh…"

"Clive Benson thought he saw your car parked on the shoulder of the road outside town around eleven."

"No," Sierra answered, casting a quick glance at Beau.

He wasn't spilling the beans about last night.

"Clive must have been seeing things, or had one too many beers at the Open Range Saloon," Duke said.

The dog tugged on his leash. "Zorro wants to walk, Dad."

Beau had yet to wrap his mind around his twin becoming a father and got a kick out of watching the father-son duo.

"See you later." Duke walked off holding Luke's hand and the dog leash.

"About last night—"

"Forget last night." Suddenly Beau didn't want to know the truth. "Will you have dinner with me tonight?"

"I have to close the diner."

"We can eat a late meal. I'll take you to Maria's Mexican Café."

Sierra wrinkled her nose. "Maria's isn't even authentic Mexican food." She stood and Beau scrambled to his feet. "Come to the diner around eight-thirty. The least I can do is feed you a meal for the trouble I caused."

"It's not much of a date if only one person eats."

"I'll have dinner, too."

"Okay, then, I'll be there at eight-thirty."

"If you run late—"

"I won't."

Sierra spun and walked briskly down the block. When she reached the corner she looked both ways then stepped onto the street. Car brakes squealed and for a split second Beau's heart jumped into his throat. The driver lowered his window and shouted at Sierra before driving off, then she hurried across the street and disappeared into the diner.

Beau's heart slid back into his chest. Dang, that woman had better pay attention to where she was going or she'd find herself in a world of hurt.

Maybe you distract Sierra.

Wouldn't that be something.

Chapter Four

"There's someone at the door, dear." Jordan's voice carried through the apartment.

Sierra glanced at her watch. Eight o'clock—Beau was on time. "I'll be right out." She'd snuck up to the apartment to change clothes for her date and had been studying her reflection in the bedroom mirror for the past five minutes. The black, short-sleeved knee-length dress flattered her full figure. The tight-fitting bosom showed off her feminine curves while the pleated skirt hid the extra few pounds she needed to lose.

Guilt pricked her for wearing a cocktail dress. She hoped to impress Beau but didn't want him believing she was interested in dating, because anything long term with the handsome cowboy was out of the question. Keeping that in mind, Sierra intended to savor every moment of the evening.

After spritzing on perfume, she left the bedroom and waltzed past her aunt, who sat on the couch reading. Molly rested dutifully at her feet. When Sierra opened the door off the kitchen…*wow*.

Beau stood on the fire escape, holding a bouquet of daisies. He wore slacks and casual shoes—she couldn't remember ever seeing him in anything but jeans and boots. Her gaze inched higher, taking in his button-down shirt and brown bomber jacket. Even in dress clothes, Beau's chiseled looks screamed *cowboy*.

He held out the flowers. "The color reminds me of your eyes."

The reference to her eyes triggered a mini heartache, but she ignored the pain and accepted the bouquet. "They're lovely." She waved Beau into the apartment, then searched through the cupboards for a vase.

"Who's here, dear?"

"Sorry, Aunt Jordan. It's Beau."

"Hello, Mrs. Peterson."

While Sierra arranged the flowers in a vase, Beau crossed the room and patted Molly on the head. "Heard my dad gave you a tour of the ranch a few days ago."

"Driving around with Joshua brought back fond memories. Seems like only yesterday that your father and I snuck off to the fishing hole on the McKinley property."

"I guess you've heard Earl McKinley leased his land to the Missoula Cattle Company."

"Joshua mentioned that was the same corporation leasing acreage from Thunder Ranch."

Her aunt's knowledge of the Adams and Hart family business pleased Sierra. She doubted that Joshua would have shared the information if he hadn't felt he could trust Jordan. For her aunt's sake and Sierra's, too, she hoped Joshua's intentions were honorable. She worried that he might be caught up in reliving the past, then once the excitement wore off and he realized his former high school sweetheart was still blind, he'd end the relationship, leaving Jordan with a broken heart and a desire to return to Florida.

"I was wondering, Mrs. Peterson—"

"Call me Jordan, Beau."

"Jordan. How far back do you and my dad go?"

"Your father pulled my pigtails in fifth grade, and from then on I was smitten."

"So you two have known each other most of your lives," Beau said.

"We went steady all through high school."

"Why'd you break up?" Beau asked.

"I went off to college."

Beau's questions sounded more like an interrogation than benign chitchat and Sierra wondered if he had reservations about his father dating her aunt. Feeling the need to intervene, she said, "Aunt Jordan, Beau and I are having dinner downstairs."

"That's fine, dear, but I need to talk to you before you turn in for the night."

"What about?"

"Scheduling an appointment with the ophthalmologist."

Since her aunt's arrival in town, not a day had passed that she hadn't hounded Sierra about seeing an eye doctor. After a few weeks the nagging had gone in one ear and out the other. Sierra would make an appointment when she was good and ready and not a minute sooner. In any event, she had no intention of discussing the private matter in front of Beau. "I'll handle it, Aunt Jordan." She walked through the living room and stopped in front of a door that looked suspiciously like a closet. "We'll use the back staircase."

"Didn't know this building had a secret passageway," Beau said.

Sierra opened the door and switched on the sconces in the stairwell. Beau followed her, closing the door behind him. Before she'd descended two steps, he clutched her arm.

"You look…hot." His gaze traveled the length of her body.

The compliment sent a rush of pleasure through her. "Thank you."

"You know what that dress says, don't you?"

Sierra couldn't think straight—not with the heady scent of Beau's cologne swirling around her head. "Wh…what does it say?"

"Kiss me," he whispered.

They hadn't sat down to eat and already Beau was making a move on her.

Go ahead. Sierra had fantasized about kissing Beau for months. Did it matter if he kissed her at the beginning of the date instead of at the end? Sierra made a feeble attempt to take the high road. "My aunt's sitting a few feet behind the door."

Beau's gaze zeroed in on Sierra's mouth. "I'm a quiet kisser."

Short of breath, she whispered, "Prove it."

His lips covered hers, then his hand settled on her hip, pulling her closer until her breasts bumped his leather jacket. Lord, the man could kiss. She followed Beau's lead, relaxing in his arms, opening her mouth to his tongue. The kiss grew more urgent, his callused hand caressing her neck…his fingers sifting through her hair.

Sierra couldn't recall the last time she'd been so thoroughly kissed and she gave herself over to the magic of the moment, memorizing Beau's scent…his taste…the scratchy feel of his beard stubble…the intimate rumble reverberating through his chest.

The kiss ended abruptly, Beau resting his forehead against hers. "You have no idea how long I've wanted to do that."

Me, too. "I think we should get off the stairs before one of us tumbles to the bottom."

"Sorry." Beau nuzzled her cheek then smoothed a hand over her hair. "I didn't mean to come on so strong."

Blushing, she descended the steps, which opened into the large pantry connected to the kitchen. When she entered the dark room Beau stopped her.

"Hold up."

With only the swath of light streaking across the floor from the passageway, Sierra was unable to see much except the shadowy outline of Beau's jaw. She waited for him to speak.

"I can't help myself." He clasped her face and his mouth inched forward.

Sierra raised her arms, intending to wrap them around his neck when the door on the other side of the pantry opened.

"Oops, sorry. Didn't mean to interrupt." Karla Dickson, the waitress who'd taken over for Irene this evening, smiled sheepishly.

"Hi, Karla." As if Beau hadn't been caught red-handed with his fingers in the cookie jar, he released Sierra and stepped into the kitchen.

Karla turned away, leaving Sierra all but forgotten in the pantry. "Duke stopped in a few minutes ago looking for you."

"I'll call him later. How about those Panthers? Your husband's team has a chance of winning the conference title this year."

"Please, no football talk." Karla groaned. "I hear enough about it at home."

Sierra shut the pantry door and faced her employee. "Any problems after I left?"

"Not a one. The tables are cleaned off and supplies

restocked. If you want, I'll run the dishwasher and prepare the coffee machines for tomorrow."

"No, thanks. I'll take care of that after Beau and I have dinner. Thanks for finishing Irene's shift today." Sierra walked Karla out of the kitchen to the front door. By tomorrow morning, the Roundup grapevine would be buzzing with rumors of Beau and Sierra kissing in the pantry.

"I'll see you on Tuesday for my regular shift," Karla said.

"'Night." Sierra locked up, then switched off the neon sign outside and returned to the kitchen where she found Beau at the stove with his finger in the gravy pot. "I'm the chef and I don't stick my fingers in the food."

"Your sirloin is one of my favorites."

She fetched two plates and dished out one small serving and one cowboy-sized serving of food. "There's wine in the pantry." The diner didn't have a liquor license, because Sierra didn't want her patrons driving home inebriated, especially when many of them lived outside the town limits. However, she kept the pantry stocked with several bottles of wine for her recipes.

Beau returned with a merlot from Napa Valley—interesting that he'd selected her favorite. She covered the bistro table in the corner with a red-and-white-checked cloth, then added two wineglasses and silverware.

A second later a pop echoed through the kitchen when Beau opened the wine bottle. He filled the glasses, then held out Sierra's chair after she brought their plates to the table. "Shall we dim the lights?" he asked.

As much as she yearned for a romantic atmosphere, Sierra worried she'd make a fool of herself if she could see only a few inches in front of her nose. "I'd prefer to keep the lights on. I like to see what I'm eating."

"Must be a chef thing." Beau sat down and raised his wineglass. "A toast."

"To what?"

"To beautiful women who can cook." He touched the rim of her glass with his own.

Sierra enjoyed watching Beau wolf down his food. He mumbled praise between bites while she contemplated how best to explain her odd behavior yesterday. As much as she wished for her life to go on as if everything were normal, she could no longer pretend her vision problems would disappear.

"What's the matter?" Beau clasped her hand, preventing the fork from swirling her mashed potatoes.

"I'm a little distracted."

"Ouch."

Sierra hadn't meant to offend him, but before she expressed her regret, he released her hand and patted his stomach. "That was the best meal I've eaten—" he grinned "—since my last visit to the diner."

"You haven't been in the past few days." Who cared if he guessed she'd kept track of his visits?

"It's not because I haven't wanted to. I added extra rodeos to my schedule."

"How long do you plan to compete?"

He pointed his fork at her. "I know what you're thinking—I can't rodeo forever. I guess thirty-two is old for a bull rider."

"You're in great shape for thirty-two." Her eyes twinkled.

Glad Sierra approved of him, Beau said, "I'd like to make it to the NFR before I hang up my rope."

"Will you get there this year?"

He shook his head. "Don't have enough points." If Duke had quit rodeo in the spring instead of in July, Beau might have been able to win enough rodeos to make the cut.

Sierra wiggled in her chair. She hadn't stopped fidgeting since they'd sat down to eat. Was she upset about the kiss? *No.* She'd participated fully and would have allowed him to kiss her again if Karla hadn't interrupted them.

"I—"

"Before you say anything," Beau said. "Are you involved with another man?"

Her eyes widened. "I wouldn't have kissed you if I was."

"Last night...I thought...well, it crossed my mind that maybe you were waiting in your car to meet with a lover."

"Why would I wait alone on a deserted road after dark?"

"Roundup's a small town. People gossip. If you wanted to keep a relationship private..." The more Beau talked, the dumber he sounded.

"Sorry to disappoint you, but the reason I was stranded had nothing to do with a lover's rendezvous."

Feeling foolish for jumping to conclusions, he chugged the remainder of his wine.

After a stilted silence Sierra set her fork aside. "Have you paid any attention to the rumors about me?"

"I didn't know you were a hot topic of conversation." He grinned. "Not that a beautiful woman like you shouldn't be talked about." His comment failed to make her smile. "I've been too busy with rodeo to listen to gossip."

Twice Sierra opened her mouth to speak but stopped.

"Whatever it is, it can't be that bad."

"I'm sorry. It's difficult to talk about."

He held her hand, encouraged when she didn't pull away.

"The reason Aunt Jordan showed up unexpectedly this summer and moved in with me is because several of her old friends told her that I've been acting...weird."

"Weird?"

"I'm having trouble with my eyesight."

"You need glasses but you don't want to wear them," Beau said.

"I already wear contacts."

"Oh." Did she mean her vision problems were more serious than needing a new prescription?

"I don't see well in the dark."

Ahh...now he understood her wanting to leave the kitchen lights on.

"And my peripheral vision isn't so good, either."

Beau recalled eating at the diner and attempting to flirt with Sierra a couple of months ago, but she'd marched past his booth as if she hadn't seen him—evidently she hadn't.

"Is that why you spent the night in your car, because you couldn't see well enough to drive home in the dark?"

"Yes."

Beau was baffled that she hadn't been truthful with him. "I offered to give you a lift into town."

"In retrospect I should have accepted your help, but I didn't want to trouble you."

"It's not like the diner was out of my way." There was more to this than Sierra not wanting to inconvenience him, but Beau didn't want to ruin the mood by pushing the subject.

"I'm sorry I lied last night. You've probably figured out I'm a little stubborn."

"A little?"

Sierra lowered her gaze to her lap. "It was nice of you to return and wait with me until morning."

"Would have been more fun if you'd joined me in my truck."

A blush spread across her cheeks. "I'd appreciate it if you didn't tell anyone about this."

He wondered why she was so bashful about her eyesight failing. "We're a close-knit community. Some of your customers would be upset if they knew you needed help but didn't ask for it."

"Please, Beau." She shook her head. "I don't like sharing my private business."

"I understand…you being a flatlander and all."

"Hey, I spent summers in Roundup when I was a kid. That makes me a semi-native."

"I'll give you that." Discussing her eyesight obviously made Sierra nervous, so Beau changed the subject. "Are we having dessert?"

"Of course." She opened the commercial refrigerator. "Peach cobbler or German chocolate cake?"

"I'll have the cobbler," he said. Sierra dished out a heaping serving for Beau and a stingy one for herself.

"Don't tell me you're one of those women who's on a diet all of the time." He liked—*really* liked—Sierra's curves.

"I have a habit of sampling the food when I cook, which makes maintaining my target weight virtually impossible."

"You look great."

Sierra laughed.

"I'm serious. You're perfect."

"You always acted a little shy when you came into the diner." She smiled. "I didn't expect you to be so forthright." Her gaze clashed with Beau's and he felt a connection to Sierra that went deeper than physical attraction. He hoped she felt it, too, because he definitely wanted to get to know her better. On the other hand, she appeared eager to end the evening when she checked her watch for the fifth time.

"I'll help you clean up." Beau didn't want to leave, but he also didn't want to overstay his welcome.

"Guests don't wash dishes."

"Sierra?"

"Yes."

"Go out with me again."

"I can't."

There hadn't been a moment's hesitation in her answer and Beau's gut twisted. "Is it because of the kiss?" His plan to move slowly with Sierra had been blown to smithereens on the back staircase. "Did I come on too strong?"

"No, I enjoyed your kiss."

The knot in his stomach loosened but not much.

Sierra collected the dirty dishes and placed them in the sink. "My life is hectic, Beau. Running the diner seven days a week takes a lot of time and then with my aunt visiting…"

Her voice trailed off and Beau had a hunch she was trying to persuade herself that she wasn't interested in dating. "We don't have to rush things." When she remained quiet, he said, "You're a beautiful woman, Sierra, and I've been trying to catch your attention for months." He tipped her chin, forcing her to make eye contact. "The money I've spent on meals at the diner could have paid for an Alaskan cruise."

Instead of making her smile, his comment drew a deep sigh from her. "You should have picked the cruise, Beau."

He tucked a strand of red hair behind her ear. "Why?"

"I'm not looking to get involved with anyone."

When she didn't elaborate, he backed off, but not all the way. "You're busy, but so am I. If I'm not riding in rodeos, I'm helping with the cattle and bulls at Thunder Ranch." He paused, waiting for her to look at him. "I'd like to spend time with you whenever we're both free."

"You mean we'd see each other as friends?"

Friendship was a good place to start. "Yeah. Friends."

"Okay. I'd like to be friends with you, Beau."

Feeling the need to leave before he said or did something to make her change her mind—like kiss her—he grabbed his jacket from the chair.

Sierra followed him out of the kitchen. He stopped at the lunch counter and pulled two napkins from the holder. "Got a pen?"

"Sure." She handed him the pen from next to the cash register.

He wrote his cell number on one napkin. "What's your number?" She recited it. Beau wanted a good-night kiss so bad his mouth watered. "Sierra?"

"Yes."

Before he lost his senses, he asked, "You ever been to a rodeo?"

"When I was a little girl my parents took me to one."

"Would you like to see me ride?"

"I'd love to go to a rodeo with you. When?"

"I'll check my schedule and call you."

She brushed at an imaginary speck on her dress. "Okay."

Leave. Before she changes her mind. Beau stepped

outside into the chilly night air. "I had a really nice time."

"Me, too. And Beau…"

"Yeah?"

"Can we keep last night just between us?"

Beau dropped his voice to a whisper. "We can keep anything you like between us."

Chapter Five

"Hey, Beau!"

Beau stopped next to his truck parked outside the Number 1 and glanced up. Duke waited for a car to pass, then jogged across the street.

"How's—"

"I wanted—"

"Go ahead," Beau said.

"Thanks again for catching Zorro this afternoon."

"Happy to help." The awkward silence that followed the exchange bothered Beau. Things just weren't the same between them since Duke had quit rodeo and married.

"I stopped in the diner earlier."

"Karla said you wanted to talk to me. I was upstairs with Sierra."

The comment tugged a smile from his brother. "Did you finally convince Sierra to go with you?"

"We had dinner together."

"Congratulations."

Beau wasn't sure congratulations were in order after Sierra had proposed a friends-only relationship.

"Heard you won in Rock Springs," Duke said.

"McLean misses you."

"McLean's an ass. I'm glad you beat him." Duke scuffed the toe of his boot against the sidewalk.

"I entered the Badlands Bull Bash next month."

"I heard. Dad got a call from Nelson Tyler Rodeos this afternoon."

Nelson Tyler Rodeos had a reputation of running top-notch events. "What did they want?"

"One of their stock contractors had to withdraw his bulls because of a fever in the herd. They asked Dad to bring Bushwhacker and Back Bender to the Bash."

Their father and aunt must be ecstatic over the news. "If Bushwhacker has a good showing he might get an invite to the NFR." Beau wished he and not a bull would represent Thunder Ranch in Vegas at the end of the year, but Bushwhacker's value would greatly increase with NFR experience and that meant more money for the ranch. "I guess I'll be helping Dad haul the bulls to South Dakota unless you plan to ride along." Beau had been doing most of the livestock hauling since Duke had gotten married and his father had begun chasing after Jordan Peterson.

"I'll check my work schedule, then I'll see if Angie has any plans that weekend."

"Since your wife thinks so highly of rodeo, I'm sure she'll find something to keep you at home."

Duke curled his fingers into fists. "Watch what you say about Angie."

Ah, hell. What was the matter with him—provoking his brother? Beau's emotions were tied in knots over Sierra's insistence that they remain friends and he was taking his frustration out on his brother. "Sorry. I was out of line."

Duke, always quick to forgive, didn't make an issue

of Beau's wisecrack. "Dad said you're serious about making a run for the NFR next year."

"I am."

"If you don't let anything get in your way—" Beau assumed *anything* meant Sierra "—then you've got a good chance of going to Vegas." His brother spoke from experience; when Angie came along, Duke had lost his interest in rodeo.

"I'd be away from the ranch more often," Beau warned.

"I'll do what I can to help Dad with the cattle and bulls."

Duke had extended an olive branch—why was it so dang hard to accept it? "I won't be making a run for anything if Dad decides to retire."

"Did he bring up the subject with you?"

"I mentioned it."

"What'd he say?"

"He said he'd be happy sitting on his keister all day."

"It's her fault." Duke pointed to the apartment window above the diner.

"What's Sierra got to do with Dad retiring?"

"Not Sierra, her aunt. Jordan's got Dad acting like a lovesick fool."

"I guess you'd know all about that lovesickness stuff." Beau flashed a crooked grin. Heck, if he played his cards right, he might have a chance to make a fool out of himself over Sierra.

"This isn't funny, Beau."

"Funny or not, I know why Dad's smitten."

"Why?"

"Jordan and Dad were high school sweethearts."

"How long has it been since Jordan lost her husband?" Duke asked.

"Not sure. A few years, I'd guess."

"Then why did she wait this long before returning to Roundup?"

"Jordan didn't come back to see Dad. She's here to spend time with Sierra." Beau rubbed his cold hands together.

"I couldn't care less who Dad dates, but he called me this afternoon while I was on duty and wanted me to contact Ace and ask him to check on one of the bulls."

"He could have called Ace himself," Beau said.

"Of course he could have, but he said he needed a haircut before he stopped in to visit Jordan and he didn't want to get stuck on the phone chatting with Ace about ranch problems." Duke shoved a hand through his hair. "I'm getting tired of Dad expecting us to pick up the slack every time he runs off to be with his lady love."

"Yeah, well, be prepared for Dad handing off more responsibility the deeper he becomes involved with Jordan."

"We already do our fair share—more so you than me—but I've got a family to look after now," Duke said.

"Maybe we're worrying for nothing. One of these days, Dad's true colors will shine through and Jordan will see he doesn't know the meaning of the word *compassion*."

"Since you're chasing after Sierra, keep your eyes and ears open around Jordan."

"For what?"

"If you hear about either of them talking marriage, let me know. I need to prepare myself and Angie for the possibility of having to spend every day off at the ranch."

"If it comes to that, we'll ask Aunt Sarah to hire another ranch hand," Beau said. "She can pay the cowboy out of Dad's retirement."

Duke chuckled then his face sobered. "You'd better watch yourself with Sierra."

Beau's hackles rose. "Why's that?"

"If you hurt Sierra, you'll not only have to answer to her aunt but Dad, too."

"No one's going to hurt anyone." Not if Beau had his way.

Duke's cell phone beeped and he checked the text message. "Duty calls. Talk to you later." He headed across the street to the jailhouse.

Beau hopped into his truck and started the engine. While he waited for the heater to warm the cab he identified the nagging twinge that always gripped his stomach when he talked with Duke. *Jealousy*. His brother appeared happier than ever in his roles as deputy sheriff, husband and father. Beau closed his eyes and envisioned him and Sierra married with kids of their own.

Be careful what you wish for…

It would be so easy to lose himself in Sierra, then end up like his brother—allowing a woman to stand in the way of winning an NFR title. Beau refused to let that happen. He was determined to focus on finishing out the year on a high note both in rodeo and his personal life. He'd win at the Bash and he'd win Sierra.

LAUGHTER FILLED THE diner and Sierra cringed at the happy sound. It was Wednesday afternoon and expectant mothers Dinah Wright and Flynn Hart had come in to appease their cravings for sweets. A few minutes later Leah Hart, Angie Adams and Cheyenne Sundell with her twin daughters had arrived and joined the group.

Steeling herself, Sierra carried a tray of water glasses

to their table. "You all appear to be in good spirits," she said.

Flynn rubbed her large belly. "I'm hoping your carrot cake will take my mind off how fat I'm feeling."

"You don't know what fat is until you've carried twins," Cheyenne said as she brushed a strand of hair from her daughter Sadie's face. The little girl jerked her head away, but her sister Sammie refused to sit anywhere but in Cheyenne's lap.

"Carrying a baby is the easy part," Leah said. "Giving birth…now that's when things get tricky."

"After helping mares birth their foals, I think we have it easier in the delivery room," Angie said.

Dinah grimaced. "Please, no childbirth stories. I just want to eat my dessert so I'll be in a better mood. Austin says I'm grumpy all the time."

Sierra steadfastly ignored the ache in her heart as she waited for the chitchat to die down. "Okay, Flynn's having a slice of carrot cake, what would everyone else like?"

"I'll take the apple pie," Dinah said.

"Make that two slices of apple pie," Leah added.

"I'll have a blueberry muffin." Cheyenne glanced at her daughters. "The girls will share a piece of chocolate cake."

"Oh, what the heck. I'll have the carrot cake," Angie said.

"Coming right up." Sierra smiled then hurried away. After passing along the dessert orders to Karla, Sierra stepped into the kitchen to check on the beef Stroganoff. "Irene, when you finish unloading the dishwasher, would you please set the water to boil for the noodles?"

"Sure."

"I'm going to check on my aunt." Instead of taking

the back stairs, Sierra left through the delivery door, which opened to the parking lot behind the diner. A cold gust of wind slapped her in the face. Yesterday, the temperature had hit fifty degrees—darn near spring-like. This morning she'd woken to plenty of sunshine but she doubted the temperature had made it out of the low forties yet.

She lifted her face to the sun and breathed in deeply, hoping the crisp air would freeze out the anxiety she'd felt the past few days. Three days had passed—almost passed—and Beau had yet to contact her about going to a rodeo with him. She'd give anything to watch him ride, but she didn't dare drive too far—Saturday night's fiasco had proven the boundaries of her world were shrinking with each passing day.

Maybe Beau changed his mind about being your friend.

Sierra should have told Beau the whole truth about her eyesight and not just that she had trouble seeing at night. Pride and vanity had coaxed her to fudge about the seriousness of the disease. She'd wanted Beau to view her as a healthy, young woman—not a woman doomed to a life of darkness.

"Where's your jacket?" Beau came around the corner of the building. His grin rivaled the sun, chasing away Sierra's melancholy. "Irene said you'd gone upstairs to check on your aunt."

"I was on my way," Sierra said.

"I dropped by to ask you to a rodeo this Saturday." He hadn't forgotten. "Where?"

"Billings."

"I'll check with Irene to see if she's willing to handle the diner."

"I don't compete until the afternoon, and there's no

snow in the forecast this weekend so we could leave as late as ten o'clock in the morning."

"Wait right here." Sierra ducked her head inside the door and asked Irene if she'd work from ten to close on Saturday. Irene was more than happy to work the entire day.

Sierra shut the door and faced Beau. "I'd love to go."

"Good. It'll be nice to have company on the drive." He touched a finger to the brim of his hat and walked off.

Where was the amorous cowboy who'd kissed her a few nights ago?

Friends, remember? Sierra had set the terms of their relationship, but a part of her yearned to throw caution to the wind just to see what might happen between her and Beau. Ah, well, a girl could dream.

"Sierra?" Jordan stood on the fire escape above Sierra's head.

"I was coming up to check on you." She climbed the steps to the apartment.

"I don't need checking on, dear. Was that Beau's voice I heard a moment ago?"

Aunt Jordan had bat ears. "Beau asked me to go with him to a rodeo on Saturday. I hope you don't mind, but I said yes." Sierra opened the apartment door and ushered her aunt inside.

"What about your eye-doctor appointment?" Jordan pulled out a kitchen chair and sat.

"What appointment?" Sierra hadn't called the eye doctor.

"I took the liberty of scheduling you an appointment in Billings with Dr. Ryder. I thought we'd stop for lunch on the way home."

Sierra counted to five as she fought her rising anger.

"Aunt Jordan, I'm capable of making my own appointments."

"Are you?"

"What's that supposed to mean?"

"You keep telling me you'll see a doctor but—"

"When I'm good and ready."

"Time isn't on your side."

"What difference does it make if I learn this Saturday or three months from now that I'm going to be blind one day?" The last thing Sierra wanted to focus on was her failing eyesight.

"What about Beau?"

The quiet question bounced off the kitchen walls, smacking Sierra on all sides. "Beau is a friend."

"A friend for now, but maybe that will change."

"My love life isn't any of your business, Aunt Jordan."

"Beau should know—"

"Beau doesn't need to know anything."

"Even if he remains just a friend, dear, he deserves to be told the truth."

A dull throb pulsed behind Sierra's eyes and she rubbed her brow. How could she make her aunt understand that she yearned for a little time to enjoy being with Beau without her vision problems standing between them? Once the doctor gave her the official diagnosis, reality would come crashing down around her and Beau would move on to another woman—one who wasn't going blind.

"Do you want me to cancel the—"

"I'll take care of it." Sierra would attend the rodeo with Beau and enjoy every second of his company. If he asked her out again, she'd make up an excuse and keeping making excuses until he got the message that friends were all they'd ever be. Needing to escape, Sierra made a dash for the door. "I'll bring up supper later."

"Don't bother, dear. I'm going out with Joshua tonight."

At least her aunt's love life appeared promising. "Have a good time." Sierra closed the door behind her and descended the fire escape, wondering if Beau was anything like his father. Would he care that she was going blind? She'd never know the truth because she wouldn't be with Beau when the day of reckoning arrived.

"LADIES AND GENTS, before we kick off our men's bull-riding event here in the Rimrock Auto Arena at the MetraPark, we've got a special treat for you."

Sierra touched Beau's thigh to catch his attention. "Don't you have to prepare for your ride?" She pointed to the cowboys standing behind the bull chutes. Beau had sat with her through several rodeo events explaining the rules and answering her questions.

"I have plenty of time. I'm riding last this afternoon."

"Today we're honored to have Shannon Douglas here with us. A native of Stagecoach, Arizona, Shannon and Wrangler Jeans have teamed up together to promote women's rough-stock events." The crowd applauded and several cowboys let loose wolf whistles.

"I didn't know women rode bulls," Sierra said.

"Not many do, but rumor has it this Shannon Douglas is one of the more talented athletes on the women's circuit."

Sierra studied the female bull rider. Even though she wore a protective vest and the customary headgear with a face mask, Shannon appeared small and vulnerable on the back of a huge bull.

"Shannon's riding Black Beauty from the Spur Ranch near Luckenbach, Texas," the announcer said. "Here's hoping Shannon makes it to eight."

The gate opened and Black Beauty burst from the chute, almost unseating Shannon. Sierra held her breath as the bull flung the cowgirl around like a rag doll. Amazingly, Shannon hung on and when the buzzer sounded she launched herself off the bull. She landed on her shoulder but quickly got to her feet and ran for the rails.

"Shannon Douglas scored an eighty-two, folks! Not bad for a girl!" Once the crowd quieted, the announcer added, "Shannon will be available for autographs in front of the VIP section after the men's bull-riding event. If you stop by and see Shannon, she'll enter your name into the Wrangler drawing for free merchandise."

"I'd better go," Beau said. He smiled at Sierra, his brown eyes warming when his gaze dropped to her mouth. "How 'bout a good luck kiss?"

Friends...remember? The warning went unheeded, and she leaned forward, pressing her mouth to Beau's, the contact sending a bolt of heat through her body. His tongue slid sensuously across her lower lip, but the instant she relaxed her mouth he pulled away.

"I should warn you that the congratulatory kiss after I win is a whole lot hotter."

"I can handle the heat, cowboy..." she teased. "If you win."

"Oh, I'm gonna win." He tapped his finger against the brim of his hat then took off for the cowboy-ready area.

Sierra pressed her tingling lips together as the loud music and raucous fan noise faded into the background. She was amazed at how easily Beau had slipped through her defenses. They were playing with fire, and the pesky voice inside her head dared Sierra to inch as close as possible to the flames without getting burned.

Relaxing in her seat, she enjoyed the rodeo until Beau's name was announced, then she gripped the armrests and sent up a silent prayer to the rodeo gods to keep the cowboy safe.

"Turn your attention to gate four. Beau Adams is the final ride of the day and he's coming out on Warrior, a descendant of the famed Houdini from the Circle T Ranch in Oklahoma. Folks this bull spins right out of the gate. Adams is in for a jolt!"

Sierra's gaze latched on to Beau as he wrapped the bull rope around his hand. She was relieved to see he'd worn the protective gear he professed to hate. Without warning, the gate opened and Warrior charged into the arena, his powerful kicks attempting to unseat Beau. Sierra gasped when the bull came dangerously close to the rails, but Beau clung to the animal.

The bull ride played out in slow motion…as if Beau and the bull were partners in a cowboy ballet of wild bucks, tight spins and wicked twists. Sierra was awed by the sheer power and beauty of Beau's body as bull and man became one violent burst of energy.

The buzzer sounded and Sierra held her breath, waiting for Beau's dismount. He dove for the ground, landing on his belly in the dirt. He lay still for an agonizingly long moment before struggling to his feet. The bullfighters distracted Warrior and Beau jogged to the rails.

"Folks, that's only the second time this season Warrior has been ridden to eight! What do the judges think of Adams's ride?"

The fans gaped at the JumboTron waiting for the

score to flash across the screen, but Sierra's attention remained riveted on Beau. Several cowboys slapped his back and shook his hand. When he removed his face mask, he glanced toward the stands. She waved her arms wildly and he grinned the moment he caught sight of her.

"Eighty-seven! Beau Adams beat Pete Monroe by one point! Congratulations, Adams!"

Sierra joined the fans in honoring Beau with a re-sounding round of applause. Proud of his accomplishment, she made her way out of the stands and down to the cowboy-ready area, where she promptly put the brakes on when she witnessed a blonde woman throw her arms around Beau's neck.

Friends...remember?

To heck with that. Sierra marched toward the pair. Beau might not be her cowboy forever, but he was darn sure her cowboy for today.

Chapter Six

"For a minute, I thought Duke was riding that bull." Melanie Kimball released Beau from her hug. "You must be a late bloomer."

"Looks that way." Beau studied his pretty former girlfriend, relieved he felt no twinges or surges of attraction to her. "How've you been?"

"Good." She stuck out her lower lip in a playful pout. "Maybe a little lonely."

Still no twinge…yeah, he was definitely over Melanie.

A cough caught his attention. "Sierra." Beau didn't have a chance to introduce the women before Melanie spoke.

"You must be the reason Beau's winning." Melanie offered her hand and Sierra hesitated before shaking it. "I'm Melanie Kimball, Beau's ex-girlfriend."

"Sierra Byrne."

"Nice to meet you, Sierra."

"Sierra owns the Number 1 Diner in Roundup," Beau said.

"That was quite a ride your cowboy gave today," Melanie said.

Sierra's gaze glanced off Beau's face before returning to Melanie. "This is my first time watching Beau compete."

"Really? Boy, could I tell you stories about him and his brother." Melanie frowned. "Speaking of Duke, why isn't he here?"

"Duke retired from rodeo." When Melanie's mouth hung open, Beau explained. "He's married now and spends his time apprehending bad guys and raising his seven-year-old stepson."

"I never pictured Duke the marrying kind." Melanie's mouth twitched. "You on the other hand…" A rowdy group of cowboys caught her attention. "Gotta go," she said. "Nice meeting you, Sierra."

Beau escorted Sierra through a maze of fans to the rodeo secretary's office where he collected his winnings. Since their run-in with Melanie, Sierra had remained quiet. Before they left the arena, he pulled her aside. "I'm sorry."

"For what?"

"If Melanie made you feel uncomfortable."

"She didn't." Sierra's blue eyes shone with sincerity.

Relieved, he asked, "Would you like to browse the vendors before we leave?"

"That's okay. I've seen enough."

Before they exited the MetraPark, Beau bought coffees for the road. Once they left the parking lot, Sierra spoke. "Mind if I ask you a personal question?"

Fearing she wanted to discuss Melanie, Beau attempted to distract her. "I bet you want to know how many buckles I've won." Her answering smile was weak at best, and Beau's stomach clenched.

"Melanie seems like a nice girl. Why did the two of you break up?"

"She's from northern Montana. The long-distance relationship took a toll on us and we grew apart."

Beau glanced across the seat and caught Sierra watching him. God, he loved her eyes…so big and round and blue. He wondered how many other men had fallen into their warm depths and drowned.

"Why didn't one of you move closer to the other?" Sierra's question snapped Beau out of his trance. He'd better focus on his driving or he'd run them off the road. "We're both from ranching families. When we're not on the rodeo circuit, we're herding cattle, hauling bulls or cutting hay."

Expecting a follow-up question, Beau remained silent. When none came, he asked, "Were you involved with anyone when you lived in Chicago?"

"Ted and I dated almost two years before my parents died and I moved to Montana."

When Sierra didn't elaborate, Beau pushed for details. "Did you and Ted try a long-distance relationship?"

"We did. Ted thought after spending a winter in Montana I'd pack my bags and return to the Windy City."

"Chicago winters are nothing to brag about."

"True, but spring and summers along Lake Michigan are warmer than here."

"What happened when spring arrived and you didn't leave Roundup?" he asked.

"Ted stopped calling."

Teddy-boy's loss. "I'm sorry." He wasn't, really, but it seemed like the right thing to say.

"In the end, everything worked out for the best. Ted's law practice and family are in Chicago. He's happy there and I'm happy here." Sierra's attention shifted to the milling cattle in the distance.

"That's the fall calf crop." Beau slowed as he approached a line of cattle trucks parked on the shoulder. Portable pens had been set up to contain the young cows.

"Are the animals on their way to the slaughter house?"

"No, the calves are being shipped south to feedlots for the winter. Once they fatten up they'll land on someone's dinner table."

"I cook meat all the time, but I prefer not to think about how it arrives at the diner."

Beau didn't mind talking beef, but he'd rather learn more about Sierra. "I heard you went to a famous cooking school in Chicago." He hadn't heard—he'd asked Irene where Sierra had learned to cook so well and the waitress had shared everything she knew about Sierra's catering business in Chicago, including where Sierra had gotten her education.

"I studied at the CHIC. The school was part of the Le Cordon Bleu program in France. I credit my mother with nurturing my interest in cooking. She taught me the basics at a young age."

"You must miss your parents," he said.

"Very much."

"I remember the afternoon their plane crashed. Half the town rushed up to Twin Peaks to search for them, but…" He silently cursed. Why the hell had he brought up the deaths of her parents?

"It's okay, Beau." Sierra touched his arm. "I find it comforting to know so many people cared about my parents."

Roundup was a tight-knit community and those

who'd searched for her parents had also eaten at Sierra's diner once it opened, ensuring her business thrived.

"I for one am glad you took those fancy food classes," he said. "Growing up without a mother was tough enough, let alone Duke and I having to eat our father's cooking. His specialty was anything that could be made in the microwave."

"Then I'm glad I helped expand your palate."

"Whoever puts a ring on your finger is going to be one lucky, well-fed man."

Sierra's smile disappeared and Beau wondered at her reaction. Was marriage a sensitive topic with Sierra? He checked the dashboard clock—six-thirty. They'd eaten a hot dog at the rodeo but that was five hours ago. "There's a burger joint about fifteen miles up the road that serves great onion rings."

"I'm not really hungry. If you don't mind, I'd rather head home and check on the diner."

"Sure." Beau swallowed a curse. He'd been hoping to spend more time with Sierra—that she wanted to cut their day short was a huge disappointment. A few minutes before eight o'clock he pulled into the parking lot behind the diner. Before he'd shifted the truck into Park and unsnapped his belt, Sierra had opened her door and hopped out. Sticking her head into the cab she said, "Thanks for the lovely day. And congratulations on winning first place."

Panicking, he said, "Wait. I'll walk you to—"

"No need. I'm going straight to the kitchen to get a jump start on tomorrow's menu." The door shut in Beau's face. Stunned, he stared out the windshield at Sierra's retreating figure. When the back door of the diner closed behind her, Beau shook himself out of his stupor. Sierra owed him a victory kiss and he wasn't leaving until she gave him one.

He rapped his knuckles on the back door of the diner, and a moment later Irene's face appeared. "Hello, Beau."

Right then Sierra walked into the kitchen, carrying a plastic tub of dirty dishes. She froze. "Did you forget something?"

Beau stepped into the kitchen, aware that Irene eavesdropped as she pretended to search the refrigerator. "No, you forgot something," he said.

"I did?"

"You forgot to give me my victory kiss."

The fridge door closed and Irene made a hasty exit from the kitchen.

Beau moved across the room, took the tub of dishes from Sierra and set it on the counter, then cupped her face with both hands and locked gazes with her. "I warned you earlier that a victory kiss is a whole lot hotter than a good luck kiss." He rubbed the pad of his thumb across the fleshy part of her lower lip. Did she want his kiss as badly as he wanted to give it to her? He got his answer when she swayed forward, her breasts bumping his chest.

He pressed his lips to hers, building steam slowly. When he slid his tongue inside her mouth she trembled and he crushed her to him. Their breathing grew hot and heavy, and somewhere in the midst of all the noise they made, Beau felt Sierra purr. Emboldened by her response, he cupped her breast, his thumb caressing her nipple, before freeing the button on her blouse. The loud gasp that followed startled Beau and they broke apart. What the hell was he doing—trying to undress Sierra in the middle of the kitchen where her employee could walk in on them?

Sierra stood in stunned silence, her eyes wide, her breathing ragged. She looked so pretty with her hair mussed, her cheeks flushed and her lips swollen. Feeling as if he was on the verge of losing control again, Beau backed toward the door. "Better fix your lipstick." He stepped outside and filled his lungs with cold, crisp air, which did nothing to calm his aroused state.

The apartment door above his head opened and Jordan Peterson stepped outside with Molly.

"Hello, Mrs. Peterson. It's Beau, ma'am."

She descended the steps with the dog. "I thought I told you to call me Jordan?"

"Yes, ma'am…Jordan." Beau waited at the bottom of the stairs, wanting to make sure the older woman didn't slip.

When she reached the pavement, she said, "I'm glad I ran into you."

"Why's that?"

"Join me while I walk Molly."

"Sure."

"I need you to do a favor for me," Jordan said.

"Okay."

"Are you free next Wednesday?"

"I'm not competing in a rodeo if that's what you're asking."

"Would you be able to drive Sierra into Billings to see her eye doctor?"

Beau recalled Sierra's explanation for why she'd spent the night on the road and assumed visiting the ophthalmologist had to do with her not seeing well in the dark. "What time is the appointment?"

"Ten in the morning."

An early appointment would allow Sierra to make the drive back to Roundup before dusk fell. Maybe Jordan was matchmaking, in which case Beau would gladly cooperate.

"Tell Sierra I'll pick her up at eight-thirty."

Molly found a place to do her business and Jordan pulled a plastic grocery bag from her pocket and handed it to Beau.

"I get to do the honors, huh?" After he picked up the mess, he asked, "Where do you want me to toss this?"

"I'll throw it away." She took the bag from Beau and they walked back to the parking lot.

"Beau?"

"Yes?"

"Did Sierra have a nice time today?"

His lips still warm from Sierra's kiss he said, "Yes, she did."

"Good. She needs to get out and do things like that more often."

They stopped at the garbage bin and Beau lifted the lid. After Jordan threw the bag inside, he said, "I'd better head back to the ranch."

"Your father left a few minutes ago. You might catch up with him on the road."

Great. Beau wondered what chores had been neglected while his father had hung out with his girlfriend. "Have a nice evening, Jordan."

The drive to Thunder Ranch wasn't nearly long enough to figure out what was going on with Sierra, Jordan and the infamous eye appointment he'd been dragged into. Instead of heading home, Beau turned onto Thunder Road and drove to the main house. He'd drop off his winnings and ask his aunt if she believed his father was going through a phase or if his intentions toward Jordan were serious, and the family had to reconfigure the work load to make up for his father's slacking off. Beau parked in the ranch yard then took the front porch steps two at a time. He knocked once before letting himself into the house.

"Aunt Sarah? You home?"

"In the kitchen, Beau."

"Something smells good." He waltzed into the room and gave his aunt a kiss on the cheek.

"Butterscotch cookies. Suddenly I have all these grandchildren, and I can't keep up with my baking."

Even though his father insisted Aunt Sarah was wearing herself out catering to all the rug rats in the family, Beau figured the kids took his aunt's mind off the ranch's financial situation and her worry over Tuf. He reached for a cookie, but she swatted his knuckles.

"They haven't cooled."

"I won in Billings today." Beau set the check on the counter and his aunt peered at the amount.

"Good gracious. You keep this up, and we'll be debt-free in no time," she teased.

"Speaking of Midnight—"

"Don't you start in on me, young man."

"Start what?"

"Pleading for Midnight to return to rodeo. Colt's pestering is driving Ace crazy and it's not difficult these days to set Ace off with Flynn's due date approaching."

"Is he worried about Flynn's health?"

"Like all expectant fathers Ace hopes she has an easy delivery, but he's also nervous about becoming a father."

"Why? He filled Uncle John's shoes without missing a beat. Unless he's worried about being too overprotective." Beau's father sure hadn't been. He'd subscribed to the parenting philosophy of sink-or-swim.

"Nothing wrong with taking care of your own, and Ace certainly does that job well."

"No argument there." Beau moved aside when his aunt slid a cookie sheet into the oven. "Some horses shouldn't be held back and Midnight's one of them."

She snorted.

"C'mon, Aunt Sarah. You've seen that horse in action. He lives for rodeo."

"I won't argue that Midnight loves competition, but we can't afford for him to get injured."

"Back Bender and Bushwhacker have had a heck of a season on the bull circuit and they haven't even peaked. Another year of competition and I bet they both make it to the NFR and bring us top dollar in breeding fees."

"God forbid, but if anything happens to Midnight and we can no longer breed him, we're going to need those bulls to cover his loss."

"We're taking Back Bender and Bushwhacker to compete in South Dakota next month. Why not enter Midnight into the competition?"

"Midnight's been out of rodeo for a long time." Aunt Sarah handed Beau a cooled cookie. "Who's going to work with him? Ace is busy with his vet practice. Colt and Duke have kids and families to look after." His aunt had intentionally left out Tuf.

"What about me? I'll go a few rounds in the ring with Midnight."

"And if you get hurt, then you've ruined your chances of winning at the Bash."

"No worries. It's just a couple go-rounds in the corral. If Midnight looks like he's not a hundred percent ready to compete, then we don't take him to South Dakota."

His aunt's gaze dropped to the check on the counter. "Okay, but no one is to know you're practicing with Midnight."

"My lips are sealed."

His aunt playfully shoved a whole cookie between Beau's lips. "You be sure to keep that mouth of yours full and don't let our secret leak out."

Beau grinned, chewed twice then swallowed. "I might need a few more cookies for the road just so I'm not tempted…."

She stuffed cookies into a Baggie then handed it to Beau. "Aunt Sarah, what do you know about Jordan Peterson and my dad?"

"Mostly what everyone else in town knows…that they dated in high school and broke up because Jordan left for college."

"Dad keeps his feelings close to the vest, but do you think he was really shaken up over their split years ago?"

"I don't know, honey. I was five years younger and wrapped up in my own life. Why?"

"Did you know Dad's been seeing a lot of Jordan lately?"

"How much is a lot?"

"Every day."

His aunt's eyes rounded. "I had no idea things had gotten that serious between them."

"We might need to think about hiring another ranch hand."

"Why?"

"Dad's been passing off his chores to me and Duke, and we're having a tough time handling our own responsibilities and covering for Dad, too."

"I'm glad your father's found someone he cares for," his aunt said. "I'll speak with Royce and Harlan. Maybe they can pick up some of the slack."

Royce and Harlan already did the work of four men

and it was hardly fair to ask more of them without offering a pay raise. Beau doubted his father considered how his actions affected others.

Aunt Sarah nudged his side. "Speaking of old and new flames..."

No way was Beau sticking around for an inquisition about his relationship with Sierra. "Gotta run. Thanks for the cookies."

"Chicken!" The accusation chased Beau through the house and out the front door.

"SIERRA, MAY I speak with you for a moment?"

Most days, her aunt waited until ten before making an appearance in the diner, but the clock on the wall read eight-thirty. Sierra didn't mind the interruption, but this morning the diner was busier than usual because members of the high school booster club were conducting their monthly meeting over breakfast. She ushered her aunt behind the register. "What is it?"

"Please don't be mad at me, but I took the liberty of scheduling you an eye appointment with Dr. Ryder for 10:00 a.m. today."

Shocked, Sierra said, "I can't leave in the middle of all this—" she spread her arms wide "—craziness."

"I asked Karla to cover for you and I'll do my best to help."

As if on cue, the diner door opened and Karla waltzed in. She smiled at Sierra then disappeared into the kitchen. "You shouldn't have called Dr. Ryder's office and—"

"If I had left it up to you, you'd have never made the appointment."

Lest she become the subject of gossip for the remainder of the day, Sierra lowered her voice. "I'm not going."

"You have to."

Embarrassed by her childish behavior, yet too scared to care what her aunt thought of her, she whispered, "You can't make me." She wasn't ready to face reality.

"Beau's waiting outside for you."

She spun toward the window. Beau leaned a sexy hip against the grille of his truck and waved. "How could you, Aunt Jordan?"

"How could I what, dear?"

"Ask Beau to drive me?" He was the last person she wanted with her when the doctor conveyed the bad news.

"I thought you two were friends."

"We are, but he doesn't have time for this kind of thing."

"Friends make time for each other. If he hadn't been able to accompany you today I'm sure he would have said so."

Sierra glanced at Beau and automatically her fingers pressed against her mouth as she recalled the victory kiss he'd claimed after the rodeo last weekend. She'd gone to bed every night since dreaming about that kiss. "Fine. I'll go."

She escaped upstairs to the apartment. After powdering her nose and applying lipstick, she collected her coat and purse and marched through the diner and out the front door.

"I'm sorry my aunt put you on the spot and asked you to drive me into Billings. I'm capable of getting there and back on my own."

"I know that."

"Then why did you—"

"Because I'll take any excuse to be with you." Beau's

slow, easy smile warmed her blood even as she thought his words weren't something a *friend* would say.

What did it matter? After today, Beau would no longer be interested in friendship much less anything else.

Chapter Seven

What was taking so long?

Almost two hours had passed since Beau sat down in Dr. Ryder's waiting room and Sierra had been whisked away by a nurse. In that entire time, no other patients had arrived or left the office. Aside from the receptionist at the check-in desk and the nurse who'd escorted Sierra to the exam room, the clinic remained eerily quiet.

What kind of eye appointment took two hours? Had the doctor performed some kind of procedure on Sierra's eyes? Beau rose from his chair and paced the professionally decorated room, stopping to stare at the wilderness painting hanging on the wall. The grizzly bear in the picture made him guess the location was northwest Montana or Glacier National Park. Beau had been to the famous park once with his brother and father, but a spring snowstorm had forced them out after only a few days in the area.

Beau's stomach growled and he continued pacing. He was on his third lap around the room when voices drifted down the hallway. A moment later Sierra appeared in the doorway. Her eyes were puffy—had she been crying? He moved closer and brushed the pad of his thumb against her cheek. "Those beautiful baby blues are okay, aren't they?"

Tears pooled in her eyes and Beau panicked. "We're out of here." He escorted her from the office and straight into the elevator across the hall. They rode in silence to the lobby then stepped outside into the chilly air and bright sunlight. Whatever had taken place inside the exam room hadn't been good and Beau floundered, wondering what to do first—ask questions or give Sierra time to pull herself together? He voted for the second option.

"Let's grab a bite to eat." He helped her into the truck then drove to a Mexican restaurant called the Cantina, which looked like a dive but had excellent food and a cozy, dark atmosphere that allowed for plenty of privacy. Beau glanced at Sierra, but she sat in stony silence. Feeling helpless, he reached across the seat and took her hand. She surprised him when she threaded her fingers through his and squeezed.

The strong urge to protect Sierra proved to Beau that his feelings for her were deepening quickly and he told himself to proceed with caution. He was under a lot of pressure—granted it was self-imposed—but he had to remain focused on his goal to win the Bash if he intended to begin next year's bull-riding season on a positive note.

When they entered the restaurant, he asked the hostess to seat them at a table in the corner. A waitress delivered tortilla chips and salsa then took their drink orders, promising to return in five minutes.

"The chicken enchiladas and pork tamales are good," Beau said.

Sierra didn't open her menu. "You pick for me."

The waitress set their drinks on the table then tapped a pen against her order pad. Beau chose the enchilada dinners for both of them. Left alone while they waited for their food, he hoped Sierra would tell him what the doctor said, and her continued silence tied his gut in knots. She looked devastated and he wanted to hug her. Had her vision deteriorated to the point where she could no longer drive? Or had the doctor told her that contacts weren't an option anymore and she had to wear glasses from now on?

"You don't have to talk about it, but I'm a good listener," he said.

"I'm ashamed to admit I'd hoped if I ignored the symptoms, the disease would go away."

"What disease?"

"Fuchs Endothelial Dystrophy. The cornea swells, which causes problems like tunnel vision, glaring, sometimes a halo effect and blurriness." She sighed. "I just didn't want to believe I'd inherited the same disease as my aunt."

Beau's lungs tightened. "Jordan's…blind."

"Blindness is the final stage of the disease."

Stunned, Beau asked, "There's no cure?"

"A corneal transplant might be an option down the road."

The band squeezing his chest loosened. There was hope. "Are there medications that slow the progression?"

"No. As the disease worsens the doctor prescribes medicated drops and ointments to ease the pain."

Their meals arrived and they ate in silence, Beau barely tasting the food. He wanted to slay Sierra's dragon, battle the disease for her, but he couldn't. The powerlessness he felt at not being able to protect someone he cared about was new to Beau and he didn't like it. Not one frickin' bit.

He opened his mouth to tell Sierra there were worse

things in the world than going blind but reconsidered. He'd tried that speech when bullies had teased Duke because of his stuttering, and all he'd gotten for his effort had been a punch in the gut from his brother.

Wanting to cheer her up, Beau suggested, "Why don't we stay in Billings and shop for Christmas gifts."

"I'm not in the mood." Sierra understood exactly what Beau was trying to do—take her mind off the doctor's diagnosis. She'd known for a while now what the official verdict would be, but she'd clung to a smidgeon of hope that maybe…just maybe her vision problems had been the result of some other issue that was curable. Fear suddenly gave way to anger—a deep, burning rage that made her want to raise her fists toward the heavens and scream at the unfairness of life.

"Have you been to the movies lately?"

As Sierra stared at Beau's mouth, the raw fury that had control of her body melted into a yearning urgency that left her breathless. Images of her and Beau making love spun through her mind, feeding an overpowering desire to live in the moment and forget about tomorrow. Embracing the newfound feeling of recklessness, Sierra vowed to live life to the fullest while she still had her sight—starting today.

There were so many things she'd dreamed of doing but the clock was ticking on her eyesight. Right then she decided to create her own personal bucket list, and who better than Beau to help her kick off her pledge to live in the moment? She reached beneath the table and caressed his thigh.

"There is something I'd like to do." She leaned close, her breast bumping his arm. "Let's get a motel room."

Beau stared, dumbstruck, and Sierra suppressed a giggle. The thought of making love with Beau felt right and good, and Sierra refused to consider the consequences. She wanted to lose herself in Beau and live as if there were no tomorrow...no next week...no next month. No next year. Before Beau had a chance to respond to her suggestion, the waitress arrived with their check. He paid cash for their meal, then escorted her outside and straight to his truck. His silence continued as he gripped the steering wheel so tightly his knuckles whitened.

She shifted closer and played with a strand of his hair. "Please, Beau."

"We shouldn't."

"We should." The longing in his gaze made her tremble. Why was he fighting his feelings? She nuzzled his neck, flicking her tongue against his warm flesh. He smelled like sandalwood and musk. Sierra's excitement fizzled when Beau started the truck and headed north on the highway.

The trip to Roundup was the longest of her life. Beau pulled into the parking lot behind the diner shortly after 9:00 p.m. and insisted on escorting her up to the apartment. Sierra wasn't raising the white flag yet. She veered away from the fire escape and entered the diner through the delivery door. Standing on the threshold she faced Beau.

Ever the gentleman, he leaned in to kiss her cheek, but Sierra turned her face and their mouths bumped. Flinging her arms around his neck, she kissed Beau as if she were marching off to war. She slipped her thigh between his legs and pressed herself against him, rejoicing in the hardness that nudged her hip. She knew the moment she'd won—he grasped her face and thrust his tongue inside her mouth. While tongues dueled, Beau cupped her breasts, squeezing softly.

Please, Beau...for tonight be the bright light in my life.

He inched her farther into the kitchen then shut the door, the quiet click of the lock echoing through the room. The soft glow of the security lights in the dining room spilled beneath the kitchen door, outlining Beau's body. The thrill of a secret encounter surged through Sierra, feeding the reckless frenzy inside her. Beau removed her coat, tossing it to the floor. Sierra kicked off her shoes and helped Beau out of his jacket. Shirts followed.

"This is crazy." His fingers released the hook on her bra, then his hand cupped her bare breast and brought it to his mouth.

"Don't stop."

Beau tugged Sierra's slacks off and lifted her onto the stainless-steel countertop. "Are you protected?" he asked.

"No," she huffed in his ear. "Please tell me you have a condom."

"My wallet." While Beau kissed a path down her neck, Sierra reached behind him and pulled the wallet from his pants pocket.

There was no turning back now.

CRAP. HAD THEY really made love on the countertop in the diner's kitchen? Even as Beau struggled to comprehend what had just transpired between him and Sierra, he couldn't resist nibbling her ear. When he pulled back and gazed at her face, her mouth widened in a satisfied smile then she playfully pushed him away and buttoned her blouse before grabbing her slacks from the floor. Jeans bunched around his ankles he turned his back and straightened his own clothes. He'd never done anything like this before and didn't know what the heck to say.

Sierra, I'm sorry I let things get out of hand? Or what he really wanted to say...*Sierra, let's do that again.*

Shoot, she was the one who engineered this...this... tryst. He'd tried to be noble and resist her advances, but he was just a guy—a guy who'd been fantasizing about making love to Sierra for months.

She cleared her throat and he faced her, relieved she smiled. "We should talk about this," he said.

"No worries, Beau. I don't expect things to change between us."

She didn't? Why the hell not? "I don't understand."

"People have sex all the time. It doesn't have to mean anything."

A queasy feeling settled in the bottom of his gut. He hadn't a clue what was going through Sierra's mind. Maybe he should leave. They both needed time to absorb what had happened between them.

"You're okay?" he asked.

"I'm fine." She unlocked the door and stood back.

He slipped on his coat. "You're sure—"

"Positive." She held out his wallet.

When his boots hit the pavement, she said, "Good night" and shut the door in his face.

What the hell? Beau had the weirdest feeling Sierra had just used him for sex.

AFTER BEAU LEFT, Sierra washed up at the kitchen sink, wiped off the counter with disinfectant spray—twice— then made her way up the back staircase to the apartment. When she opened the door she was caught by surprise—her aunt and Beau's father were locked in a passionate embrace. "Oops." Sierra retreated into the stairwell. "I didn't mean to interrupt."

"I should be going," Joshua said.

After a few seconds, Sierra entered the apartment. She offered an apologetic smile but Joshua's gaze skirted her face. "There's a quarantined bull at the ranch I need to check on."

Jordan grasped Joshua's hand and she followed him into the kitchen. Sierra thought it was sweet that the older couple always held hands. After Joshua shrugged on his coat, her aunt lifted her face and there wasn't a moment's hesitation before Joshua kissed her.

"Good night, Sierra," he said.

"'Night, Joshua."

After another quick kiss, Joshua left and Aunt Jordan closed the door. "Sierra?"

"In the living room."

Jordan sat down on the sofa.

Sierra would have preferred to put off this conversation until tomorrow and retreat to her bedroom where her memory could relive her passionate lovemaking with Beau, but her aunt had waited all day to hear the doctor's diagnosis.

"You were right," Sierra said.

"How far has the disease progressed?"

"Far enough that I've been warned never to drive at night." As if she didn't already know that.

"Did Dr. Ryder give you any idea when you'll…"

Sierra said the word *blind* in her head but still refused to accept the offensive word. "Dr. Ryder said there was no way to determine when I'd lose my sight." But he had predicted that it wouldn't be for many years and Sierra was grateful for that small blessing. "There's a chance that I might be a candidate for a cornea transplant."

"Then there's hope."

Yes, but Sierra wasn't wasting another day waiting

around for hope. From now on, she intended to live each day to the fullest.

"Now that you have an official diagnosis, you can prepare yourself."

How did anyone map out a life in the dark? "I don't care to think about that right now, Aunt Jordan."

"You need to plan for the future, dear. There are ways you can make the transition easier."

Sierra appreciated her aunt's advice, and in due time she'd devise a battle strategy, but not now. "Forget about me, let's talk about you," Sierra said. "How's your love life?"

A soft smile flirted with the corner of her aunt's mouth. "Joshua and I realized that neither of us has ever stopped caring for each other."

"But you married Uncle Bob."

"Yes, and I loved Bob, but when I went off to college I left a piece of my heart with Joshua. Every now and then through the years I thought of him and wondered what would have happened if I'd remained in Roundup and married him."

"You wouldn't have become a dancer or earned a college degree or traveled the world with Uncle Bob."

"That's true. And I credit your uncle with helping me conquer my fear of going blind. With his guidance, I remained independent despite the loss of my eyesight."

"How did he help you?"

"Because of your uncle's military background, he viewed my eventual blindness as a war—one he determined I'd win. If not for his insistence that I learn to fend for myself and do everyday tasks without his help, I wouldn't be able to get around on my own as much as I do."

"You don't believe that if you'd married Joshua he'd have helped you live a fulfilling life?"

"Joshua would have become impatient with me and stepped in to help when he shouldn't have. I'd have become too dependent on him." Jordan sighed. "Your uncle was a soldier. Not even my tears or pleading for help swayed him to give in to me."

"Sounds like Uncle Bob used the tough-love approach."

"Because of Bob's determination, I've enjoyed a rich, full life since I lost my sight."

"How is Joshua handling your blindness?"

"Better than I expected, but he's changed since we dated."

"Changed how?"

"He's quieter." Her aunt laughed. "He was such a prankster when we went steady. Playing tricks on me, then when I'd become frustrated with his jokes, he'd surprise me with a poem or a bouquet of wildflowers." Jordan's smile weakened. "I think his wife's death deeply affected him."

Selfishly, Sierra hoped Joshua had gotten over the death of his wife and was ready and willing to commit to Jordan. "How did his wife die?"

"Her car careened off the road during a snowstorm. The twins were only two at the time, but thank goodness they weren't in the car with her. Frankly, I'm surprised Joshua never remarried. Raising his sons alone must have been trying at times."

"Does Joshua ask about your life with Uncle Bob?"

"No. That's why I've been hesitant to bring up his wife."

Testing the waters Sierra said, "I guess it doesn't matter if you're just friends."

"We're more than friends, Sierra."

"So…you might be willing to relocate permanently to Roundup?" Sierra crossed her fingers.

"It's a definite possibility. Life goes by fast. I don't want to regret not reaching for happiness when it's within my grasp." Her aunt tapped a finger against the couch cushion. "Speaking of men who make us happy… how do you feel about Beau?"

If what had transpired between herself and Beau a few minutes ago was any indication, then Sierra definitely had the hots for the cowboy. "Beau's a nice man—" and sexy as heck "—but all we're ever going to be is friends." No way would Sierra allow her feelings for Beau to deepen, knowing in the end that there was no future for them.

Sierra faked a yawn then said, "I'm going to turn in early."

"But we should discuss setting goals for—"

"Not right now, Aunt Jordan. Sweet dreams." Sierra slipped into her room and shut the door. She sat on the bed and tears flooded her eyes. Making love with Beau had been both a thrill and a curse. A thrill in that he'd made her feel things she'd never thought she'd feel with a man, and a curse because now she knew she'd never have what she yearned for—a husband and children of her own.

STILL IN A state of shock over what had transpired between him and Sierra, Beau parked outside the barn and went into his workshop. He might as well get started on the saddle for Jim Phillips. Keeping his hands busy would calm his jumbled thoughts. He hung his coat over the stool next to the workbench then selected a medium-sized fiberglass frame from his stockpile and placed it on the wooden saddletree. For extra reinforcement he attached a steel plate from the pommel to the cantle beneath the tree.

Next, he added the stirrup bars—three-inch wide brackets with a movable catch set into the bar. While he hammered the bar into the proper shape, his memory replayed the scene at the ophthalmologist's office.

He didn't want to admit that learning Sierra might one day go blind had shaken him to the core. He couldn't imagine those beautiful blue eyes of hers left in the dark. He stopped pounding the bar and closed his eyes.

What would it be like if one day he woke up and the sights that had been familiar to him all his life… saddles…cattle…the mountains…bulls went dark? Beau wasn't sure he could handle that. How would he cope if he couldn't make his saddles? His chest physically hurt when he thought of Sierra's love of cooking and the possibility that one day she might have to give it up.

If Beau were to lose his sight, activities he'd taken for granted—walking to the barn, showering or answering the door—would become potential hazards. He sifted through his stash of leather stirrups until he found a pair he liked, then sat on the stool and stared into space. How had he allowed things between him and Sierra to get out of hand—sex in the diner kitchen? What if someone had walked in on them? The idea of getting caught stirred Beau and he squelched the X-rated images that popped into his mind. Sierra gave no sign that what they'd shared had meant anything to her except sex, and no reason to believe their lovemaking had changed their relationship.

What the heck was their relationship anyway? He'd thought they'd started dating then all of a sudden they'd skipped getting-to-know-you and had gone straight to doing the down-and-dirty.

In retrospect, he wondered if Sierra's actions were a direct result of the eye doctor's diagnosis. He'd heard stories of people who reacted to bad news in bizarre ways and he had no intention of holding Sierra's actions against her. To Beau's way of thinking, the best thing for them to do as a couple was take it one day at a time. He liked Sierra a lot—no sense worrying about the future when there was nothing he could do to change the course of her eye disease.

Chapter Eight

Friday afternoon Beau left the equipment barn and spotted his brother's blue Ford barreling up the drive. Almost an entire week had passed since Beau and Sierra's sexy interlude in the diner kitchen. He hadn't phoned Sierra or dropped by the diner in five days, believing they needed a cooling-off period. Boy, had he been wrong. Keeping his distance from Sierra had only fueled his erotic dreams.

"Aren't you supposed to be at work?" he asked when Duke stepped from the truck.

"Dinah said I deserved a day off, so I thought I'd see if you or Dad needed my help."

Beau continued walking to the barn, Duke falling in step alongside him. "You should have asked Dinah if you could have tomorrow off, instead."

"Why's that?" Duke stopped short when Beau put on the brakes and faced him.

"I could use an extra hand hauling the bulls to Three Forks."

"Bushwhacker and Back Bender are old pros. They won't give you any trouble."

"Asteroid's going, too. He's competing in his first rodeo and there's no telling how he'll behave."

"Sorry. Dinah's driving into Billings with Aunt Sarah on Saturday to shop for baby furniture."

"Guess Royce or Harlan will have to help out." The ranch hands wouldn't mind. They enjoyed meeting up with old acquaintances at the rodeos.

"Why isn't Dad going?" Duke asked when they entered the barn.

"He's taking Jordan to a ballet in Bozeman."

"Ballet?" Duke frowned.

"Yeah, that was my reaction, too."

"Jordan's blind. Why would they—"

"I guess she performed with a dance company in California years ago."

"The two of us need to talk to Dad. He can't keep throwing extra responsibilities at us," Duke said.

"I'll leave you to do the talking," Beau said, even though he knew his brother wouldn't confront their father. Duke was the peacemaker in the family so it would be left up to Beau to square off with the old man if push came to shove. "Dad's ticked off at me for seeing Sierra."

"I don't understand."

"He warned me away from getting involved with her," Beau said.

"Seriously?"

"He's worried I'll do something that will sabotage his relationship with Jordan."

Duke shook his head. "He's gone off the deep end."

Beau entered the room at the back of the barn where a twenty-five-year-old bucking machine was stored and flipped the light switch.

"I still don't get what Jordan sees in Dad. He's not exactly the kind of guy who sticks by your side through thick and thin," Duke said.

"Maybe Jordan's softened him up."

"I guess Dad's finally gotten over Mom."

"Looks that way." Beau believed their father had been so heartbroken over the death of his first wife that he hadn't been able keep any photographs of her around the house. The few times Beau had asked about his mother, his father had changed the subject. Beau straightened the mats beneath the bucking machine—mats that had been worn thin by years of use.

Duke laughed.

"What's so funny?"

"Remember the night we snuck out here to try the machine after Dad warned us to keep away from it?"

"We were seven at the time, weren't we?" Beau wiped his dusty hands on his jeans.

"Dad woke up and discovered our beds empty—"

"—and Uncle John was so pissed at him for not checking the barn before he roused the whole ranch to search for us." Beau chuckled.

"I have a confession to make," Duke said.

Before their falling-out over the summer, Beau and his brother used to discuss everything and anything. Missing that connection with his twin, Beau said, "You know I can keep a secret."

Duke stared longingly at the bucking machine. "I miss riding bulls."

Since when? Duke had been one hundred percent certain that he was finished with rodeo when he'd married Angie.

"Don't get me wrong. Angie and Luke are the best things that ever happened to me and I don't regret walking away from rodeo."

"Then what is it you miss about riding?"

"The adrenaline rush."

"Don't you still get that feeling when you see Angie in her birthday suit?"

Duke shoved Beau playfully. "Brothers aren't supposed to talk about their sisters-in-law that way."

"Says who?" Beau teased.

"I see I'm gonna have to teach you a lesson in respect." Duke narrowed his eyes.

"You and what army?"

Duke lunged at Beau, wrapping him in a bear hug. He lifted his brother off his feet then tossed him to the mats. Beau seized Duke's ankle and down his twin went, Beau rolling out of the way before Duke crashed on top of him. The brothers grunted, groaned and laughed as they wrestled. Several minutes later, and out of breath, Beau hollered, "Stop!"

"Giving up already?"

"Hell, no. There's a better way to settle this." Beau hopped to his feet. "We'll have ourselves a ride-off."

"You're on." Duke started the machine, the old motor groaning and squeaking. "It's been a while, so I get a warm-up ride."

"Real cowboys don't need practice runs," Beau taunted.

Duke hopped onto the machine and after catching his rhythm, he said, "Turn it up a notch."

Arm high above his head, Duke's body swayed with the machine. Duke was all about finesse while Beau's performances were choppy. There were pros and cons to both ways of riding, but Beau conceded that his brother *looked* better busting bulls than he did. Beau flipped the machine to High without warning and the sudden jolt sent Duke to the mats.

"Cheater."

"Watch how the professionals do it." Beau slowed

the machine, hopped on and waited for Duke to saunter over to the wall and switch gears. Duke flipped the machine to High and Beau flopped around like a fish on dry land. He relished the fight—even if it was with a machine. Duke cheered him on, reminding Beau of days gone by when they'd traveled the circuit together.

When Beau remained on the bull a full minute, Duke shut off the machine. "You're ready to compete tomorrow."

"We should do this more often. Bring Luke next time, and we'll teach him how to ride."

"I just got married. I'm not looking to give Angie a reason to divorce me."

While the brothers threw the tarp over the machine, Beau's cell phone chimed with a text message. "It's Aunt Sarah. She wants us up at the main house."

"Anything wrong?" Duke asked.

"She didn't say. You go ahead. I'll lock up here." After the rash of robberies over the summer, Beau and his father no longer left the property unsecured when they weren't close by. Beau made sure all doors were bolted then hopped into his truck and headed to his aunt's. When he arrived, the driveway was filled with trucks. Then he spotted the patrol car and decided it must be serious if Dinah had driven out to the ranch while on duty. Beau entered through the back door and stepped into a kitchen full of arguing people.

Aunt Sarah noticed him first and offered a nervous smile. "Beau's here." The announcement quieted the group. "Royce and Harlan went out to check on the pregnant mares a short time ago and discovered Miss Kitty miscarried," his aunt said.

No wonder the family was upset—Miss Kitty, a former bucking bronc, was a proven breeder and had been carrying Midnight's foal. Ace paced the tile floor. "I checked Miss Kitty two days ago and she showed no signs of being in distress."

"This isn't your fault." Aunt Sarah patted her eldest son's arm. "Mother Nature works in her own mysterious way."

Beau felt bad for Ace. His cousin looked miserable. No one worked harder than Ace to keep Thunder Ranch afloat and its animals healthy.

"Midnight hasn't settled down since he returned from Buddy Wright's ranch this past summer. Maybe it's time we discuss our options," Aunt Sarah said.

Ace spoke first. "One option is that we sell Midnight and cut our losses."

"Midnight stays." Colt's chin jutted. "I'll put more hours in working with him."

"You've busted your backside on that stallion for months, and he still won't have anything to do with a dummy mount," Ace argued.

"He'll come around," Colt said.

"Even if you work with Midnight 24/7 all through the winter, there's no guarantee he'll relax enough that we can trust him again with the mares next spring," Ace said. "By then, we'll have invested money we can't afford to lose in his care and upkeep. And we don't know if any of the other mares we put him with will miscarry in the coming months."

"Let Midnight earn his keep." All eyes shifted to Beau. "If Midnight's allowed to rodeo, he'll bring in enough money to pay for his feed while Colt continues to work with him."

"Beau's right," Colt said. "Midnight's a competitor. He'll settle down if he has a chance to get rid of his excess energy."

"I'm more worried about Mom than Midnight." Dinah hugged her mother. "No horse is worth the trouble if the stress affects your health."

"My heart is fine, sweetie." Aunt Sarah spoke to the group. "We were all hoping Midnight would be our lucky charm, but we have to do what's best for the ranch and for Midnight."

"I'm with Ace on this one," Duke said. "Midnight's had his chance and he's not living up to our expectations."

"Joshua." Aunt Sarah studied her brother. "You've been awfully quiet. What do you think?"

"I'd like to see Midnight go for broke," he said. Beau wondered if his father wasn't also referring to his relationship with Jordan Peterson.

"What do you want to do, Mom?" Colt asked.

Aunt Sarah straightened her shoulders. "Before we put Midnight on the auction block, he deserves another chance." The room erupted into arguing. Aunt Sarah opened the utensil drawer, removed a spatula and smacked it against the counter until everyone was silent. "We keep Midnight until next spring. If he's still unpredictable and difficult to control at that time, then he goes."

The kitchen cleared out quickly, leaving Beau alone with his aunt. "Does this mean Midnight can definitely compete in the Badlands Bull Bash?"

"Yes."

"When are you going to tell Ace?"

"I'm not."

Beau's eyes widened.

"I'll leave that up to you."

"Do you want me to sneak Midnight off the property to practice?"

"Not unless you want the others to alert Dinah or Duke and begin another statewide search for the stallion."

"I'd planned to ride Midnight this Sunday after I return from Three Forks."

"That's fine." She tugged his shirtsleeve. "Be careful, Beau. I don't want either of you hurt."

"Wait and see, Aunt Sarah. Midnight will be a different horse once he's in the arena bucking off cowboys."

"I pray you're right. We could use the money and a little hope around here."

Beau wondered if the *hope* his aunt referred to had more to do with his cousin Tuf's estrangement from the family than a spirited horse with a stubborn streak.

SIERRA WAS DOWN on her knees, stocking paper goods behind the lunch counter when the sleigh bells on the diner door jingled. She glanced at her watch—7:45. Go figure—a late customer would happen along right before closing time. "Be with you in a moment!" She set aside the bundle of napkins and climbed to her feet, then sucked in a surprised gasp. Beau sat at the end of the lunch counter.

He hadn't called her since they'd returned from Billings a week ago and…and…she slammed the door on the image of her and Beau having sex on the kitchen counter. Good grief, not an hour in the day passed in which she didn't recall the steamy scene.

"Got a minute?" he asked.

Relieved that the last patron had left a few minutes ago, Sierra moved from behind the counter and flipped the Open sign to Closed. When she turned away from the window, she bumped into Beau and automatically pressed her palm to his chest to regain her balance. The heavy thump of his heart beneath her fingertips made her pulse race. Beau placed his hand over hers, pinning her fingers to his shirt.

She couldn't think straight, standing this close to him.

"I'm riding in Three Forks tomorrow. Come with me."

"I can't. Irene's husband is sick and she's staying home to take care of him."

"I'll help out." Karla emerged from the kitchen, flashing a mischievous smile. Had she been eavesdropping behind the door?

Beau grinned. "Karla's willing to cover for you."

"Aunt Jordan—"

"Your aunt is going to a ballet in Bozeman with my father."

"That's right. I forgot." Sierra's face heated.

"I can run the diner," Karla said. "You've already prepared tomorrow's special. It's just a matter of heating the food."

Before Sierra could come up with a plausible excuse to skip the rodeo, Beau kissed her. A slow and steady I'm-in-no-rush kiss—right in front of her employee.

"When should I be ready?" The question slipped from her mouth in a satisfied sigh.

"Six-thirty." Beau nodded to Karla then left the diner.

"Things are moving right along between you and Beau," Karla said.

Oh, joy. With Karla in charge of the diner tomorrow, Sierra and Beau would be the topic of conversation among the Roundup regulars.

"YOU SURE YOU don't want something to eat or drink?" Beau asked.

"No, thanks. I'm fine." If he bugged her about food

one more time Sierra would smack him. She and Beau
sat in the stands at the Three Forks Rodeo, watching
the barrel-racing event. At least his former girlfriend
wasn't competing—that took some of the sting out of
Beau's hovering.

Was it her imagination or had he morphed into a
cowboy hen? All day he'd stood too close or gripped
her elbow at the oddest times as if expecting her to suddenly walk into a wall. As she'd feared, learning about
her eye disease had made Beau more vigilant around
her. The last thing she wanted was to be smothered.

"Isn't it time for you to ride?" Bull riding was the
final event of the rodeo—thank God, because she
needed a little breathing room before they drove back
to Roundup.

He leaned close and whispered, "Can't leave without
my good luck kiss."

As if she could stop herself... Sierra brushed her
lips across his. "Good luck." *And please don't get hurt.*

Her gaze followed Beau out of the stands. There was
a huge part of her that yearned to latch on to him as if
she hadn't a care in the world, but she doubted he'd be
willing to live in the moment with her as she tackled
the items on her bucket list. As much as she wanted to
be with Beau, he was a take-charge kind of guy who'd
only get in the way of her goals.

"Ladies and gents, it's time to kick off America's
most extreme sport—bull ridin'!"

The raucous noise that followed the announcer's spiel
drowned out Sierra's introspection and she turned her
attention to the JumboTron. Images of past bull rides
flashed across the screen while the Garth Brooks song
about the sport of rodeo blasted through the arena.

"This afternoon we've got eight foolhardy cowboys

ready to do battle with the meanest critters on God's green earth."

The fans stomped their boots on the metal bleachers, tugging a smile from Sierra—she enjoyed watching the crowd as much as she did the actual events. Switching her attention to the cowboy-ready area, she searched for Beau—not an easy task for her eyes when all the cowboys wore colored shirts that blurred together in a kaleidoscope of bright hues. She'd asked Beau why none of the men wore yellow and he'd told her that yellow was the color of cowards. Cowboys and their kooky superstitions.

When Sierra noticed Beau climbing onto the back of a bull, she edged forward in her seat and sent up a silent prayer for his safety.

"Turn your attention to gate six and Beau Adams from Roundup, Montana. After a slow start earlier in the year, this cowboy's had a steady run of good luck the past few months. We'll see if Adams has what it takes to tame a bull called Tankulicious. Tank hails from the Norton Palmer Ranch in Nebraska."

Beau slipped in his mouth guard. His teeth clanked together more times in eight seconds than a hockey player's did during an entire game and if he intended to kiss Sierra again, he didn't want to damage his pucker. Next, he adjusted his Kevlar vest then shoved his hat down on his head. A cowboy hat might not look like much protection but a good quality hat could mean the difference between a bruise and a gash.

Closing his eyes, Beau emptied his mind of all thoughts except Tank. Bull riding was twenty percent talent and eighty percent mental toughness. Ready as he'd ever be, he leaned over the bull's right shoulder, lifted his arm in the air and braced for combat.

The chute door opened and Tank barreled into the arena like a derailed freight train. Beau was prepared for the first buck, lunging forward over the bull's shoulders. Focusing on Tank's momentum, Beau allowed the bull to guide him into the next kick. Like a ballroom dance, Tank led and Beau followed. Neither beast nor man raised the white flag as seconds ticked off the clock. When Beau heard the buzzer, his mind switched gears and he waited for an opening to dismount.

Tank continued to buck and spin, but Beau hung on, praying the bull wouldn't yank his arm from the socket. Finally, Tank's engine sputtered and Beau took advantage of the bull's letdown. Releasing his hold on the rope, he used Tank as a springboard and launched himself through the air. He hit the ground on all fours and his hat popped off his head.

The bullfighters moved in, escorting Tank from the arena. Beau grabbed his hat and saluted the cheering crowd then blew a kiss toward the stands where Sierra sat. The camera replayed his actions on the JumboTron before turning the lens on the blushing redhead.

"There you have it, folks!" the announcer shouted. "Beau Adams becomes the first cowboy this season to ride Tankulicious to eight!"

"Don't get a big head, Adams." Royce slapped Beau's back. The ranch hand had driven the stock trailer to the rodeo, and Beau and Sierra had followed in Beau's truck.

"I ripped that ride, didn't I?" The more wins Beau tucked under his belt before the Bash in November, the more confident he'd feel going into the event. He stuffed his gear into his bag and handed it to Royce. "Will you keep an eye on this for me? I'm going into the stands to get Sierra."

"Sure."

Beau tipped his hat to the fans who acknowledged his performance as he worked his way through the rows to Sierra's seat. When he reached her, he whispered, "Come with me." Taking her by the hand Beau walked out to the concourse, then pulled Sierra aside and kissed her.

Mmm...she tasted like honey. He backed her into a dark corner that afforded them more privacy. Even though the shadows hid them from rodeo fans he kept the kiss PG-rated—until Sierra melted against him and he captured her moan in his mouth. Her eagerness sucked him in and he deepened their embrace. Someone whistled and Sierra ended the kiss, burying her face against his neck.

Her lips nuzzled his skin, and Beau imagined waking each morning with her cuddled in his arms, limbs entwined, their quiet breathing filling the room. Eventually, they'd have to start their day and open their eyes— one pair seeing...the other pair left in the dark.

The abrupt thought startled Beau and he stepped back. Cheers from the fans and the announcer's voice faded into the background as Sierra threaded her fingers through his hair, coaxing him to push aside thoughts of the future and focus on the here and now.

"That was some congratulatory kiss," he murmured.

"Better than others you've received, I hope?"

"What others?"

She playfully punched his arm.

"How would you like to watch the last few bull rides down by the chutes?"

"I'd love to see the action up close," she said.

Holding Sierra's hand, Beau led her through the throng of competitors in the cowboy-ready area. He tightened his grip, guiding her around a maze of cowboy gear bags and saddles on the ground. When they reached Bushwhacker, he kept Sierra close at his side.

"Beau," she whispered. "You're squeezing too hard."

"Sorry." He relaxed his arm around her. "Sometimes Bushwhacker kicks out in the chute." Instead of appreciating his concern, Sierra moved away from him.

Beau didn't have time to figure out what he'd done to deserve her cold shoulder when the chute door opened and Bushwhacker exploded into the arena. Just as in the previous rodeo, the bull gave his best effort and the cowboy went airborne at the three-second mark. Two rides later, Back Bender had the same success in the arena. Now it was time to see what Asteroid would do in his first rodeo.

Asteroid left the chute running. *Buck, Asteroid, buck.* The bull ducked to the right so suddenly that the cowboy landed on his rump in the dirt.

"Crap," Beau grumbled.

"What happened?" Sierra stood on tiptoe to gain a better view of the arena.

"Asteroid was a dink."

"What's that?"

"A dink is a bull that doesn't buck."

Royce approached Beau. "Looks like we've got our work cut out for us with Asteroid."

"Dad won't be happy when he hears about his performance." Beau turned to Sierra. "I need to help Royce load the bulls once they settle down."

"That's fine. I don't mind waiting."

Cowboys gathered up their gear while rodeo workers began to tear down the chutes and makeshift holding pens. Fifty yards away, a shoving match between two cowboys drew the attention of rodeo officials who broke up the fight. The cowboy-ready area was no place for a lady. "You'd better wait in the stands."

Sierra scowled.

Okay, so she didn't care to be told what to do. "Things get crazy down here after the rodeo, and I don't want you to get caught in the cross fire."

Her blue eyes turned icy. "See you later then."

Before Beau had a chance to escort her back to her seat, she stomped off. He watched her retreat, wincing when her foot tangled with the handle of an equipment bag. Thanks to the quick reflexes of a nearby cowboy who steadied Sierra, she was spared a possible injury from an embarrassing fall.

Stubborn woman.

Chapter Nine

Beau slowed the truck as he drove down Main Street in Roundup. He pulled into the lot behind the diner then turned off the engine. "Thanks for coming along today." He stared longingly at the back door of the building, hoping Sierra would invite him inside for a late-night coffee.

She grappled for the door handle. "Congratulations on winning another buckle."

He didn't care about the buckle. Why was Sierra suddenly eager to end their day? Was she still upset with him for asking her to sit in the stands while he loaded the bulls? He hopped out of the truck, rounded the hood and opened the passenger door. He offered his hand but she ignored his help and walked toward the fire escape. Damn. He didn't want to end the day on a sour note. He trailed her up the stairs and waited as she opened the apartment door, then stepped inside and gasped.

Beau's first thought was that a burglar had broken in. Bracing for a confrontation, he pushed past Sierra. The intruder turned out to be his father—locked in a passionate embrace with Sierra's aunt. "Sorry for interrupting." Beau wondered whose face was redder— his or his father's? Despite everyone's embarrassment, Beau found his father's predicament amusing. He'd never seen the old man with his shirttail hanging out and his hair mussed.

"Sierra's home." Beau's father attempted to straighten his clothes then gave up, scowling at Beau as he retrieved his coat from the back of the chair.

"I thought you'd be gone longer, Sierra." Jordan smoothed a hand down her slacks.

"I'm tired," Sierra said. "I enjoyed the rodeo, Beau, thanks for taking me." She waltzed into her bedroom and shut the door.

So much for ending the date on a positive note. "How was the ballet?" Beau asked.

"Wonderful," Jordan said.

"Bushwhacker and Back Bender both came out on top." When his father didn't inquire about Beau's ride, he said, "I won, too."

"Doesn't surprise me."

The backhanded compliment startled Beau. His father rarely praised his twins.

"Good night, Jordan." Beau waited outside on the fire escape while the older couple said goodbye. When his father stepped onto the landing, Beau grinned.

"Don't say a word."

They walked in silence to their trucks, then Beau followed his father back to the ranch. When they entered the kitchen, his dad said, "We need to talk." He filled the coffeemaker with water, flipped the switch and sat across the table from Beau.

"This is about Jordan, isn't it? You've got serious feelings for her," Beau said.

"No, this is about you and Sierra."

"What about us?"

"I thought I told you to keep your distance from her."

Swallowing an angry retort, Beau said, "What happens between Sierra and me isn't any of your business."

"Well, I'm making it mine because Jordan means..." His father's voice trailed off. He left the table and fetched a beer from the fridge.

"You just put a pot of coffee on."

"I need something stronger." His father twisted off the cap and took a long swallow.

"Jordan means what?" Beau asked.

"She means the world to me. If you hurt Sierra—"

"Last time I spoke with Jordan I got the impression she approved of me and Sierra dating." Beau struggled to understand his father's objections to his relationship with Sierra. Did a couple of dates and hot sex on a kitchen counter even constitute a relationship? "Sierra and I are grown adults capable of making our own decisions."

"Watch it, young man. You're treading on thin ice."

After the way the day with Sierra had ended, Beau was itching for a fight and his father appeared determined to oblige him. "You've got a lot of nerve assuming you know what's best for everyone when you were such a crappy dad." He expected his father to explode—when he didn't, Beau mumbled, "Sorry. I shouldn't have said that."

"No, you're right. I wasn't a good father."

Shocked his dad had owned up to the charge, the anger fizzled out of Beau. "Was it because of Mom's death?"

"I loved your mother." Then his father dropped a bombshell. "But I've always loved Jordan more."

"So you settled for Mom when Jordan left Roundup after high school."

"I held out for a while believing Jordan would come home, but she didn't."

"Did Mom know you felt this way about another woman?"

"Not in the beginning."

Oh, man, this didn't sound good. "When did Mom figure out you were still in love with Jordan?"

"Right after your second birthday."

"How?"

"She found a box of old love letters between Jordan and me, and guessed that I'd only proposed to her after I learned that Jordan had become engaged to another man."

"What did Mom do?"

"We argued and she left the house."

Beau felt light-headed. He'd heard many accounts of his mother's death from various people and family members, and all the stories had involved his mother driving in bad weather and her car sliding off the road and hitting a tree head-on.

"The fight happened the afternoon Mom died, didn't it?"

His father rested his face in his hands. "I can't tell you how many times a day I think about that moment and regret not stopping your mother from going out in that storm."

Wait until Duke heard the truth. "Did you tell Jordan?"

"No. And I'm not going to. It wasn't her fault, Beau. It was mine. I'm the one who couldn't let Jordan go all these years." The lines bracketing his father's mouth deepened and he looked every one of his fifty-eight years. "If I'd burned those letters...who knows, maybe your mother and I would still be married today."

His father had kept this secret to himself all these years and Beau couldn't imagine carrying around such a heavy burden.

"I take full blame for you and Duke having to grow up without a mother, and for that I am deeply sorry." The misery in his father's eyes conveyed his sincerity.

So many pieces of the puzzle finally fit together. Maybe later Beau would process his father's confession. "Jordan's not the same person you dated in high school. How can you be sure she's what you want this time around?"

"Jordan is the same spirited girl I fell head over heels for. The only difference is that she's blind. I'm the one who changed, and I'm humbled that Jordan still sees something worthwhile in me."

"Have you asked her to marry you?"

"No, but I've dropped several hints."

"And...?"

"She changes the subject."

"Why?"

"Jordan hasn't said as much, but I believe she's too worried about Sierra to think of herself right now." Beau remained silent and his father continued, "Promise me you'll stop leading Sierra on."

"How am I leading her on? I've taken her to a couple of rodeos. That's it." *And you've had sex with her. That's a lot.*

"Sierra's not the kind of girl you have a fling with, son."

"Whoa, hold on a minute. Who said anything about flings?" Had Sierra told her aunt they'd slept together?

"Just keep your pants zipped."

"Why should things be any different for Sierra and me? You're dating a woman who's already blind."

"That's right. I know what I'm getting into. You don't. There's no telling how long it will take for Sierra to lose her sight completely—could be a few years or three decades."

"So?"

"So...that means Sierra will be riding an emotional roller coaster for years, and that kind of stress can ruin a relationship."

"I get it now. You want me to quit dating Sierra so you can move forward with your plans for you and Jordan."

"You're making me sound selfish."

"If the shoe fits." Beau shoved his chair back and stormed out of the house. As much as his father's advice offended him, he conceded the old man was right about one thing—Beau had to decide where he stood with Sierra. He couldn't continue to ask her out on dates, flirt with her and maybe have sex with her again unless he was willing to stand by her through good, bad and blindness.

AT HALF-PAST ONE in the morning, Beau's cell phone went off. He'd thrown himself into working on the Phillips' saddle, the task taking his mind off the conversation with his father, and he'd lost track of time. He checked the number. *Duke.*

"What's wrong?" Beau asked when he answered the call.

"It's Sierra."

The blood drained from Beau's face. He'd dropped her off at her apartment a few hours ago—what could have happened between then and now that would involve a deputy sheriff? "Is she okay?"

"She's more than fine at the moment, but I doubt she'll be feeling too chipper in the morning."

"Hell, Duke, Sierra's either okay or she's not. What's going on?"

"I got a call from Ted Malone over at the Open Range Saloon. Sierra's tearing up the dance floor."

Beau had never run into Sierra at the Open Range, or any other bar in Roundup. "Are you sure it's Sierra?"

"Oh, I'm sure. I'm at the bar right now watching her line dance by herself." Duke sounded worried. "She's had an awful lot to drink, Beau. She shouldn't drive home."

Sierra had driven her car after dark? Why would she do something so reckless—even though the bar wasn't far from the diner? "I'm on my way."

"You might want to hurry."

"Why's that?"

"Some cowboy's hitting on her and it looks like she might leave the bar with him."

"Arrest her if you have to, but don't let Sierra out of your sight." Beau disconnected the call and raced from the barn. The drive to the Open Range took twenty minutes going ten miles over the speed limit and he pulled into the lot behind the bar right at closing time. Two trucks, Duke's patrol car and Sierra's SUV, sat parked near the back entrance.

Having no idea what to expect, Beau braced himself when he entered the bar. As his eyes adjusted to the dim interior, he scanned the room. Only die-hard boozers closed a bar down, but the few patrons sucking on last-call drinks appeared harmless. Then Beau's gaze shifted across the room and he spotted Sierra's image in the wall-length mirror behind the mahogany bar. She was draped like a tablecloth over a cowboy who didn't look familiar to Beau. He took a step in their direction but Duke cut him off. "Ted said Sierra's snockered."

"What's she been drinking?"

Duke grinned. "You sure you want to know?"

"Tell me."

"Let's see—" Duke counted off his fingers "—she's had a Sex on the Beach, a Between the Sheets, a French Kiss and a Screaming Orgasm. Followed by a Slippery Nipple. The drink in her hands right now is a Slow Screw." Duke checked his watch. "All since eleven-thirty when she walked into the place."

Holy crap. Sierra had gone off the deep end. Beau walked toward the couple, his boot heels sticking to the hardwood floor. He tapped the cowboy on the shoulder. "Excuse me. That's my girl you're holding."

The cowboy's glazed eyes told Beau he'd already passed his booze limit.

"Hey." The cowboy shook Sierra's shoulder. "This your guy?"

Sierra lifted her head and smiled. "Beau?"

"In the flesh."

She shook her head, then rested her forehead on the cowboy's shoulder and muttered, "I'm not his girl."

"She says she's not your girl. That makes her my girl." The cowboy tipped Sierra's chin and stared her in the eye. "You wanna go back to my place, sugar?"

The endearment grated on Beau's nerves. Aware of Duke standing by ready to intervene, he said, "She's not going anywhere with you, buddy. You're both drunk."

"Party pooper," Sierra said. She crawled out of the guy's lap and took Beau's hand. "I wanna show you something." She led him to the empty dance floor, but stopped when she noticed Duke. "When did you get here?" she asked.

"Almost an hour ago."

"Oh. You wanna dance with us?"

"I'm not really into threesomes."

Beau jabbed his elbow into his brother's gut.

"I'm going to teach Beau how to line dance." She tugged him to the center of the floor. "It's called the Tush Push." She swayed and Beau's hand shot out to steady her. She rubbed her head and looked disoriented.

"Get ready, she's going down," Duke warned.

"First, you step like this." Sierra moved left, then right, then spun and fainted dead away in Beau's arms.

"Need help?" Duke asked.

"Nope." Beau swung Sierra over his shoulder in a fireman's carry. With her fanny sticking high in the air, he marched toward the exit.

"Don't forget her purse," Ted hollered from behind the bar.

Beau switched directions and returned to the bar where the saloon owner held out the black clutch.

"Arlene coaxed Sierra to let her keep it after her third drink."

"Thanks." At least Ted's wife had looked out for Sierra tonight. Any crazy fool could have stolen her purse and she'd never have known it. Duke held the door open for Beau and followed him to his truck. Beau set Sierra in the front seat and snapped the belt around her, then shut the door.

"Appreciate you telling me what was going on with Sierra," Beau said.

"If you want, I can lock you two up for the night in one of the jail cells."

That wasn't a bad idea. If the good folks of Roundup learned Sierra had gotten hammered and spent the night in lockup she'd be less inclined to tie one on again.

"Thanks, but I'll sit with her in the diner tonight in case she gets sick."

"Good luck." Duke got into his patrol car and drove off.

Soft snores filled the cab as Beau drove down Main Street. When he parked behind the diner, he searched through Sierra's purse for her keys then turned off the truck. He stared at the fire escape, wondering if he should wake Jordan and ask her to keep an eye on Sierra. No. Beau wanted to remain at Sierra's side through the night—for his own peace of mind.

Once he'd carried her into the diner, Beau set her in a booth. She slumped over and his quick reflexes caught her right before she banged her forehead on the tabletop. He propped her against the wall next to the booth then tucked her legs beneath her before retrieving one of the plastic tubs used for bussing tables. He placed the tub in front of Sierra then put on a pot of coffee and sat in the booth with her.

The wait began. At three o'clock Sierra sat up straight and slapped a hand over her mouth. Beau moved the dishpan closer and they were off—round one of a triple-header. The next few hours were spent rinsing out the dishpan and mopping Sierra's forehead with a cool cloth. Around five in the morning he offered her a soda cracker, but she refused.

Noise woke Beau at 6:00 a.m. He shifted in the booth, the left side of his body numb where Sierra was draped across him. Her hair was a tangled rat's nest, her mascara smudged and her lips pale. She looked terrible but Beau's heart swelled with emotion. He set her aside and slid from the booth.

"Morning, Irene," Beau said when he stepped into the kitchen.

"She get plowed last night?" Irene's eyes twinkled.

"I guess you could say she had a little too much fun."

"Heard she was dancing up a storm at the Open Range."

By noon the entire town would know about Sierra's drinking binge.

"You take Sierra upstairs and put her to bed. I can manage the morning shift."

"You sure, Irene?"

"Positive. That girl works way too hard. I'm glad she's letting her hair down and enjoying herself for a change."

Enjoying herself? Sierra's reckless behavior worried Beau. What if Duke hadn't been called to the bar to check on her—would she have gone home with a stranger? The thought of Sierra waking up in another man's bed sent a surge of anger through Beau. He might not have any legitimate claim on Sierra but they'd made love, and in his mind that gave him at least a right to some answers.

Beau parked his pickup in front of his aunt's house Sunday morning at 7:30 a.m. Even though he was dead tired after watching over Sierra, he looked forward to riding Midnight. Hopefully the stallion would take Beau's mind off the crazy stunt Sierra had pulled last night.

"You ready to rock-n-roll, Midnight?" Beau stood outside the horse's stall. All was quiet in the barn—Gracie and her boys were still at church.

The stallion eyed him warily but didn't object to being led into the adjoining corral. The moment Beau released him, the horse circled the enclosure, snorting clouds of white steam into the cold morning air.

After retrieving the bareback rigging and flank strap

he'd brought in his truck, Beau returned to the corral and allowed Midnight to sniff the gear. The stallion threw his head back then raced to the opposite end of the enclosure.

The next fifteen minutes were spent rearranging the fencing panels until Beau had constructed a makeshift chute. Since he didn't have a helper, he didn't bother with a gate. The only problem with his plan was that he'd have to back Midnight into the chute; the horse might balk at the unfamiliar routine.

"Ready, boy?"

Midnight took off, bucking. His high-arching kicks would make any seasoned rodeo cowboy nervous. Once he calmed, Beau approached with the gear then walked backward toward the chute. Midnight followed him.

The sweet purr of a diesel engine met Beau's ears. Colt parked his truck in the drive. "Are you doing what I think you're doing?" he asked in a hushed whisper as he approached the corral.

"Yep."

Colt grinned when he noticed Beau's predicament. "Need a little help?"

"Looks that way."

"Got any ideas on how you're going to get that horse to back himself up?"

"Nope. You?"

"Maybe." Colt walked Midnight forward then stopped him when the stallion's back end aligned with the opening. He then placed his palm on the horse's chest and pushed firmly. Midnight didn't budge. When Colt removed his hand, the stallion backed himself slowly into the enclosure, stopping when his rump nudged the rails.

"I'll be damned," Beau said. "Think Ace'll believe this when we tell him?"

"I doubt it." Colt glanced at Beau. "Does my mom know you're working with Midnight?"

"Yep."

"She always let you and Duke get away with the same shit she raked me and Ace over the coals for."

Beau chuckled. "That's because we didn't have a mom."

"Better quit yammering and ride. Midnight won't stay in there forever."

Once they secured the flank strap and rigging around the stallion, Beau climbed the rails and settled onto Midnight's back. Satisfied with his grip, he said, "I'm ready."

Midnight didn't flinch, so Beau pressed his knees against the stallion's sides. Nothing. "What's he waiting for?"

Colt backed up slowly. "I've got an idea. Hold tight." He hurried into the barn then returned with a pitchfork.

"You planning to jab him in the butt to get him to move?"

"Ready?" Colt lifted the rake toward the top rail of the pen and clanged it against the metal.

Midnight bolted at the sound, vaulting from the chute and almost unseating Beau. He didn't have time to think about anything but hanging on for dear life. As soon as he got a little cocky, believing he might outlast Midnight, the horse went into a spin that sent Beau flying. He landed hard, but rolled to his feet, grinning. "Whew! Did you see that, Colt?"

"Don't get a big head, hoss. That was far from Midnight's best effort." Colt patted his cousin on the back. "My turn."

When the men glanced across the corral, Midnight was already standing near the chute. "He's a competitor, that's for sure," Beau said.

"He needs practice with a real chute. Next time we'll rig up something better."

"As long as Ace doesn't find out," Beau reminded his cousin.

"Don't worry, he won't."

Beau wasn't as confident that they could keep their secret from Ace. His older cousin had a sixth sense about things and eyes in the back of his head. Beau just hoped that when Ace did find out, he wouldn't blow a gasket.

Chapter Ten

By Wednesday afternoon Sierra had survived the worst of the inquiries about her excursion to the Open Range Saloon. Of course people would speculate that she'd gone off the deep end when she rarely visited the bars. Gossip aside, what bothered Sierra most about her night on the town was the fact that Beau had whisked her out of the bar as if he'd been her keeper.

Okay, so she'd found out from Irene, who'd been told by Dinah, who'd spoken to Ted the bartender, that Sierra had passed out in Beau's arms on the dance floor. And maybe she should appreciate that Beau had taken her back to the diner and sat with her through the wee morning hours while she'd tossed her cookies, but Sierra hadn't asked for Beau's help and she resented his interference.

Just because they'd had sex didn't mean they were a couple. Beau had no right to decide what was best for her. Besides, it wasn't like she was going to make a habit of partying at the bars. Her night at the Open Range had been a one-time thing—a chance to let her hair down and release the stress that had been building inside her for months. She'd already moved on from that night, making plans to tackle the first item on her bucket list.

The diner door opened and the thorn in her side

waltzed in. Beau's gaze clashed with hers and she felt her face warm—not from embarrassment but because the man was too darn sexy for his own good. She hadn't phoned Beau after she'd recovered from her hangover, because he'd been the last person she'd wanted to explain her actions to.

Regardless, she owed Beau an obligatory *thank you* even if she hadn't asked for his assistance. He took a seat at the lunch counter and she grabbed a white mug and the coffeepot. She poured his coffee then choked the words out. "Thank you for taking care of me Saturday night."

"I was surprised when Duke said you were having a rip-roaring time at the bar."

Sierra didn't care to discuss her private business in front of customers so she changed the subject. "Are you eating?"

"No. I just stopped by to see you." His mouth curved in a smile.

Even as her heart sighed, Sierra straightened her shoulders and jutted her chin. She couldn't allow Beau to sneak past her defenses because she knew there was no future for them.

"I also wanted to invite you to a rodeo this coming Saturday. It's a small event in Bridger. I won't be hauling any Thunder Ranch bulls, so I thought we'd stop for dinner afterward."

No more rodeos. The last thing she wanted was more of Beau's hovering. Besides, she already had plans for Saturday afternoon. "I'm sorry. I can't."

The sparkle in Beau's eyes dimmed. "I'll bring you straight home after I compete."

"I appreciate the offer, but—"

"I'll help Irene, Sierra." Her aunt stood by the kitchen door, wearing yellow latex gloves covered in soap suds.

Sierra held her tongue and counted to ten for fear she'd shout at everyone to back off and give her a little breathing room. "Thanks, Aunt Jordan, but no." Good grief, she'd spent all Sunday in bed with the dry heaves. She couldn't afford to play hooky for an entire day, but unbeknownst to her aunt, Sierra was taking the afternoon off.

Beau's big brown eyes studied Sierra and she almost changed her mind. The memory of their lovemaking still haunted her when she crawled into bed. Reliving the intimate moments they'd shared made her yearn for a future with Beau, but common sense intervened. She'd stick with her own plans—much safer for her heart. Sierra motioned to the menu lodged between the condiment bottles. "Let me know if you change your mind about eating." Steeling herself against the hurt look on his face, she retreated to the kitchen where she remained until Beau left.

"GOT A MINUTE?" Beau poked his head inside the door of the sheriff's department and waited for Duke to glance up from the file in front of him.

"Sure." Duke set aside the paperwork and walked over to the watercooler. "Thirsty?"

"No, thanks." Beau slouched in the chair facing his brother's desk. His ego had taken a beating after Sierra's brush-off a few minutes ago and he was too agitated to drive home. He motioned to the file his brother had been reading. "What's the latest report on crime in the area?"

"Investigating a broken window out at widow Haney's house. Dinah believes the widow slammed her storm door too hard and it cracked the glass. Mrs.

Haney claims she's been targeted by Roundup's hooligans."

"Mrs. Haney likes to stir up trouble because she's bored and doesn't have anyone to henpeck since her husband died," Beau said.

"You're right, but Dinah's got a soft heart. She'll jump through hoops for Mrs. Haney and talk to the schoolkids."

"Speaking of broken windows…remember those slingshots Dad made for us when we kids?" Beau said.

"Aunt Sarah was so pissed after we broke her kitchen window."

"And she really got riled when we told her we'd been aiming for the bird on the ledge."

"Boy, did Dad get a dressing-down from his sister."

"Joshua, if you let those boys attack innocent birds they'll be aiming at people before you know it." Beau mimicked their aunt's voice. "Who knew Aunt Sarah had a soft spot for yellow-bellied sapsuckers?"

"I don't think I said two words to Aunt Sarah for a month after Dad hid the slingshots," Duke said.

A stilted silence followed and Beau squirmed in his seat.

"Trouble in paradise?" Duke quirked an eyebrow. "If you need any advice—"

Beau scoffed. "Just because you found your better half and settled down doesn't mean you're an expert on male-female relationships." The urge to unload on Duke was tempting, but Beau wasn't used to seeking his brother's counsel. Most of their lives Beau had been the one to defend and protect Duke's feelings. Beau changed the subject to one Duke was always eager to discuss—their father. "Had a long chat with Dad the other night."

"That so?"

"I guess it was more of an argument than a discussion."

"What happened?"

"Sierra and I walked in on him and Jordan kissing." Beau grinned. "Dad's shirt was untucked."

"I've never seen Dad so preoccupied. It's like he's someone else, not the man who raised us." Duke rested his feet on the corner of the desk and leaned back in his chair. "What did the two of you bicker over?"

Beau left out the part about being warned way from Sierra—he hated to believe his own father would put his happiness ahead of his son's. Heck, it might not even matter anymore... Beau had a feeling Sierra was pulling away from him and he felt powerless to prevent it from happening. "We talked about Mom."

Duke's eyes rounded.

"Dad confessed that he never loved Mom the way he loves Jordan. He said he proposed to Mom after he heard that Jordan had gotten engaged to another man."

"Jeez. Poor Mom. Good thing she had no idea Dad had betrayed her."

"She knew."

Duke sat up straight, his boots hitting the floor with a thud. "What?"

"Mom found Dad's love letters to Jordan and figured it out on her own."

"How did Mom react?"

Beau stared at his brother for several seconds, communicating without words.

"The car accident," Duke whispered.

"They got into an argument over the letters and Mom stormed out of the house."

"Dad didn't try to stop her?"

"No."

"Unbelievable." Duke sprang from his chair and paced across the room.

"Dad feels pretty bad about what happened and he blames himself for us growing up without a mother."

"No wonder he's always been a curmudgeon. Must have been hell living with all that guilt," Duke said. "Do you think they would have stayed married if Mom hadn't died?"

"Who knows? In any event, Dad's determined not to waste his second chance with Jordan."

"Did he say they're getting married?" Duke asked.

"No, but I think it's only a matter of time before he proposes to her. I figure Dad's slacking off is going to be the norm from now on."

"I never pictured the old man marrying again, did you?"

"No." Beau hesitated, feeling awkward, then asked, "Was it tough for you to give up rodeo for Angie?"

"Not as much as I'd believed it would be. I was used to being on the road a lot and I worried I'd miss all the excitement if I stayed in one place."

"What changed your mind?"

Duke smiled. "When you love a woman with all your heart you realize pretty quick you don't want to be away from her for very long."

"And fatherhood? You were thrown into that role and didn't have much time to get used to the idea."

"I love Luke. We're kindred spirits. He's a lot like me when I was younger."

"Do you and Angie want more kids?"

"Why all the questions?" Duke asked. "You didn't get Sierra pregnant, did you?"

"Hell, no!" A flashback of Sierra's sexy sprawl on

the stainless-steel counter shot through Beau's brain and he swallowed hard. They'd used a condom... He shook his head. Sierra wouldn't have gone on a drinking binge if there had been a chance she was pregnant.

"My turn to be nosey," Duke said. "Did Sierra ever tell you what Saturday night was all about?"

Embarrassed and hurt that Sierra had shut him out after they'd made love, he said, "I don't have any claim on Sierra. She's free to party and have a good time if she wants."

"For someone who's laid back about your relationship you sure rushed to her rescue at the bar."

"I care about Sierra and wanted to make sure she got home safe." And Beau hadn't been about to let her go home with another man.

"It isn't any of my business what's going on between you and your lady love," Duke said, "but I'm going to speak my mind."

Turnabout was fair play. Beau had blistered Duke's ears earlier in the summer when his brother had quit rodeo. "I'm listening."

"Angie's a strong, independent, stubborn woman."

"So is Sierra," Beau said.

"Then beware. Don't let a woman's strength fool you into believing her heart can't be broken. The last thing Sierra needs is a man to bail on her when the going gets tough."

And the going would get tough...a little more each and every day. "Warning received." Beau headed for the door and Duke followed him outside.

"Are you riding anywhere this weekend?"

"Bridger."

"Is Dad going?"

"What do you think?"

"He's spending time with Jordan."

Beau nodded.

"He'd better not call me for help. Angie's got a fix-it list a mile long waiting for me to tackle."

"Good luck with that." Beau moseyed down the block to his parked truck. He glanced across the street as he passed the diner and watched Sierra move about the tables, talking to her customers. Maybe she needed time to come to terms with the doctor's diagnosis.

He'd give her space, but that didn't mean he had to like it.

SIERRA'S BUCKET LIST rested on the passenger seat of the car as she drove through Billings early Saturday afternoon. According to the GPS she was within a mile of the Yellowstone Drag Strip. She was nervous yet excited about her first time drag racing. Yellowstone Drag Strip advertised weekend specials, which included a half-hour instruction class, three practice runs in a race car with an instructor, then two drag races against an opponent. The package cost Sierra $350 but she didn't bat an eyelash at the amount. She spent little money on clothes and she rarely treated herself to manicures or pedicures, so she had plenty of money in her savings to finance her bucket list.

Ever since her father had taken her to a real dragracing event when she'd been a little girl, the sport had fascinated Sierra. She remembered loving the loud rumble of the powerful car engines and the incredible speed at which the cars traveled. One day in the not-too-distant future she'd have to give up her driver's license, but today she intended to race the wind.

The building came into view and the GPS directed Sierra to turn onto a frontage road, which emptied into a crowded parking lot. After finding a parking spot she entered the building and filled out a packet of forms. She fudged on the health questions—who needed perfect eyesight to steer a car in a straight line? Once she paid her fee, she was loaned a driver's suit and helmet then introduced to her instructor—a woman named Mandy. Mandy asked about Sierra's driving experience and she confessed that she'd never driven a vehicle with a larger motor than a six-cylinder engine. Mandy escorted Sierra and three others to a small classroom where they watched a video on racing safety then stowed their belongings in lockers, put on their driving suits and walked out to the racetrack behind the building.

Heart pounding with excitement, Sierra wished Beau wasn't so overprotective. She would have loved to have invited him along today so they could have raced each other on the track.

BEAU HAD JUST entered Billings when flurries hit the windshield. He fumbled with the radio until he found a weather report—sleet changing to snow with a possible two-inch accumulation—nothing unusual for late October in Montana. What *was* unusual was that the TV weatherman the previous evening had forecast clear skies with clouds rolling in after midnight and a slight chance of flurries by morning. Must be nice to have a job where you got paid whether you were right or wrong.

His cell phone rang and Beau recognized his father's number. Now what? The old man never called to ask how Beau did in his rodeos. "What's up, Dad?"

"Where are you?"

"Just entered Billings, why?"

"It's Sierra."

Beau's stomach dropped. He changed lanes then turned into a business and shifted into Park. "What's going on?"

"Jordan's worried about Sierra. She left this afternoon to go into Billings but said she'd be back by five."

Beau glanced at the dashboard clock—five-thirty. Why was Sierra in Billings? He'd thought she'd had to work in the diner all day. "Did Jordan try Sierra's cell phone?"

"Of course she did. Sierra's not answering."

Anger competed with worry. "What do you want me to do, Dad?"

"Sierra scribbled an address on a piece of paper that Irene found. Plug it into your GPS and see if she's there."

This coming from the man who'd told him to keep his distance from Sierra? Beau grabbed a pen from the glove box and used the back of a fast-food bag to write down the address his father recited. "I'll let you know what I find out." He disconnected the call, entered the information into his GPS, then left the parking lot and merged with traffic. Ten minutes later he pulled into the Yellowstone Drag Strip, figuring his father had transposed the numbers in the address.

When he stepped into the building and asked if a Sierra Byrne had been there, a young kid pointed to the exit that led outside to the track. "She's got one more race. She had trouble with her car and it put her behind schedule."

When Beau left the building, a blast of cold air hit him in the face. The snow was falling harder and the wind gusts were stronger—not the safest racing conditions. Beau searched for Sierra, but the pit area was empty. Then he heard the sound of revving engines and jogged around the side of the building where two race cars—one red and one black—gunned their engines. A woman stood on the side of the track holding a flag. God help him—was Sierra driving one of the cars?

Before Beau came to grips with the possibility, the woman waved the flag and race-car wheels spun against the slick pavement before lurching forward onto the straightaway. The black car edged out the red one as they neared the finish line, then the red car put the brakes on too hard and fishtailed. The driver over-corrected, sending the car careening into a blockade. Rubber tires spewed into the air then rained down on the car. The flag woman hurried toward the wreck.

Beau's boots remained rooted to the cement and his heart pounded so hard it hurt. Eyes glued to the red car, he held his breath as he waited for the driver's door to open. The driver emerged from the car and removed his—her helmet. *Sierra.* Beau was too far away to hear the conversation between the drivers and the instructor, but the smile on Sierra's face assured Beau that she hadn't been injured. When her gaze landed on Beau, the smile vanished and her solemn stare punched him in the gut. He retreated inside the building to wait for Sierra and for his heart to stop pounding like a jackhammer.

"What are you doing here?" Sierra asked Beau when she emerged from the locker room twenty minutes later.

Acting as if finding Sierra drag racing was an everyday occurrence took more effort than Beau imagined. He kept his distance from her, fearing if he got too close he'd hug her so hard she'd suffocate. As far as he could tell there wasn't a scratch on her, so why the heck did he feel light-headed?

"My father called when I was on my way home from the rodeo in Bridger. Your aunt was worried when you didn't answer your cell phone. Jordan wanted to warn you about the storm heading this way."

"So you had to run to my rescue?"

Rescue was a bit harsh. "Your aunt was worried."

"I don't need your help, Beau."

Okay, now he was angry. "It's dark outside and the snow's falling harder. How did you plan to get back to Roundup tonight when you're not allowed to drive in the dark?"

"I listened to the weather forecast yesterday and the snow was supposed to hold off until late tonight." She motioned to the exit that led to the track. "I didn't count on there being a problem with the race car. That delayed my start time or else I would have been on my way home well before now."

Beau was ticked that Sierra was acting as if her decision to drag race wasn't a big deal when in his mind it was a *very* big deal. She had no business engaging in activities that put her in danger. "What's your game plan now?"

"I guess I'll find a motel room." She narrowed her eyes.

"Who's going to drive you to the motel from here and bring you back in the morning to get your car?"

Her chin rose higher. "I'll take a cab," she said, then retrieved her cell phone from her purse.

"C'mon." He clutched her arm. "Let's get out of here." All he wanted was to keep Sierra safe and sound with him. He helped her into his truck then drove through Billings. The snow flurries turned to sleet, freezing on the pavement. Traffic slowed to a crawl and Beau realized there was no way he could make the drive to Roundup safely tonight. He was stuck in Billings, too.

Suddenly the driver in front of him slammed on the

brakes and spun into the fast lane. Sierra gasped and
Beau white-knuckled the steering wheel as he watched
the driver narrowly escaped a collision. Before Beau's
heartbeat returned to normal, a second car hit a patch of
black ice and slid through a red light. That driver wasn't
as fortunate. A pickup slammed into the passenger-side
door.

"That's it," Beau said when he noticed the motel
across the street. He signaled and switched lanes then
pulled into the parking lot. "We're both getting a motel
room for the night."

Chapter Eleven

"Will you call your aunt and let her know we're staying in Billings tonight?" Beau pulled behind a line of cars checking into the Holiday Inn Express. The place was filling up fast and he worried they wouldn't get a room.

Sierra pressed the speed-dial number on her phone. "Aunt Jordan, it's Sierra." Pause. "I'm fine. Beau and I are waiting out the storm in Billings."

Beau noticed Sierra neglected to tell her aunt that they were getting a motel room or that she'd been drag racing this afternoon.

"I'll be back first thing in the morning," she said.

Now that Sierra was cooperating with his plan, the anxiety in Beau's gut eased. He'd never forget the sickly feeling he'd gotten when her race car had careened into the pile of tires. At least tonight he'd have peace of mind knowing she was safe with him and not out somewhere pulling another daredevil stunt.

"Please see if Karla or Irene will open the diner tomorrow," Sierra said. "I promise. Love you, too. Bye."

"Promise what?" Beau asked after she disconnected the call.

"Aunt Jordan said to thank you for helping me—her words, not mine."

Jordan might be grateful to Beau for rescuing her

niece, but Sierra sure wasn't appreciative. Beau didn't understand this new pattern of risky behavior Sierra was engaging in, and he was clueless as to how to help her through this tough time. The one thing he knew for sure was that if she continued pulling these stunts his hair would turn gray before his next birthday. A guest exited the motel, and as soon as he drove off Beau took his parking spot.

"How did you do at the rodeo?" Sierra asked.

"Not good. Monstrosity kicked my butt." Once Beau had been thrown, the bull had continued to buck and his hoof had caught Beau on the hip. The force of the blow had sent him flying through the air a second time.

"I'm sorry."

"You should be. It was your fault I got thrown in the first place," he said.

"Me? How did I cause you to fall off the bull?"

"Cowboys don't fall off bulls…they get bucked off."

"Whatever." She waved a hand. "Why is it my fault that you lost?"

Tell her the truth. "I was preoccupied before, during and after my ride."

"By what?"

Not what—who. "I couldn't stop thinking about you."

Sierra dropped her gaze to her lap.

"If you'd agreed to go with me to the rodeo, I wouldn't have had trouble concentrating." Because he would have known Sierra was sitting in the stands while he'd been in the cowboy-ready area. Instead, he'd thought about her recent excursion to the Open Range and had worried about her change in behavior. After seeing what she was up to today he had a right to be concerned.

"Beau…"

"What?"

"Just because we…slept together doesn't mean you have a say in what I do with my life."

Her words shouldn't have hurt, but they did. He was looking out for Sierra's best interests, but anything he said right now would only upset her. He reached for the door handle. "Wait here while I check on availability."

When the truck door shut, Sierra breathed a sigh of relief. Her knight in shining armor had rescued her again and she didn't like it, not one darn bit. Her thrilling afternoon had ended on a sour note—being stuck in a motel room with Beau interrogating her wasn't on her bucket list.

Fifteen minutes later, receipt in hand, Beau drove to the lot behind the motel and parked.

"I guess they had rooms left," she said.

"Room. We got the last one."

"Double beds?"

"One king-size." He turned off the engine. "And I'm warning you right now, I starfish in bed."

"What do you mean, you starfish?" she asked when he opened her door.

"I sleep with my arms and legs spread apart."

Their room was located next to the exit on the first floor. Beau inserted the key card into the lock, opened the door and flipped on the lights. Ever the gentleman, he allowed Sierra to enter first.

"I'll call the front desk for a roll-away," she said.

"Already asked." Beau shut the door and secured the locks. "All the cots are taken." He walked farther into the room and adjusted the heater. "The desk clerk recommended the burger joint across the street. I'll head over and get us dinner."

She wasn't hungry but the scowl on Beau's face

warned her not to be difficult. "I'll have a cheeseburger, small fries and a diet cola."

"Lock up after me."

Sierra shut the door and slid the safety chain into place, then hurried into the bathroom and washed her delicates in the sink with the motel shampoo. Afterward, she spread them to dry on the heater then returned to the bathroom to shower. She raised her face to the hot spray and closed her eyes.

If anyone had told her how this day would end—her and Beau sharing a motel room and a king-size bed—she would have insisted they were crazy. As much as Beau's overprotectiveness annoyed her, she still found him sexy as sin. Thank goodness she was still upset with Beau—at least she didn't have to worry about jumping the cowboy's bones.

Sex would only complicate their relationship. Sex led to expectations. Commitment. Taking the other person into account when making decisions. Right now Sierra only wanted to worry about herself.

She finished her shower and wrapped herself in a towel. Once her skivvies dried, she'd slip on her street clothes again. Sleeping in jeans and an itchy turtleneck wouldn't be comfortable, but there was a price to pay for having too much fun. Tightening the towel she slid beneath the bed covers and turned on the TV. In a matter of minutes, she became engrossed in a cooking show and lost track of time.

A knock on the door startled her. "Just a minute!" She crawled from the bed, adjusted the towel then checked the peephole. The image in the hallway was bleary. "Beau, is that you?"

"Yeah, it's me."

Keeping the safety latch secured she peeked through

the open door. The two-inch gap provided enough light for her to make out Beau's features.

She opened the door and he stepped into the room and secured the locks. When he turned around, his eyes widened. Sierra backpedaled until her legs bumped the mattress, then she tugged self-consciously at the edge of the towel.

"I don't have a change of clothes with me," she mumbled. Beau attempted to look away, but his gaze strayed to her and Sierra silently cursed the tingle that raced through her.

"I asked the front-desk clerk for toothbrushes and toothpaste." He moved closer, tossing the travel-sized toiletries on the bed along with his duffel, then he set the fast-food bag on the table in the corner. "I carry a change of clothes with me when I rodeo in case—"

"You end up stranded in a motel room with a woman?"

"Something like that." He removed a pearl-snapped dress shirt from the leather bag and held it out to her. "This might be more comfortable to sleep in."

She clutched the material to her chest. "Thank you."

His mouth curved in a lopsided grin. "The shirt will look better on you than it does on me."

Sierra slipped into the bathroom, buried her nose in the cotton material and inhaled. The garment smelled like detergent and a little like Beau's sandalwood cologne. The shirttail ended an inch above her knees and covered all the important body parts. When she stepped from the bathroom she caught Beau in front of the heater, her pink panties dangling from his finger.

"Forget something?" he asked.

She snatched the silk from him and returned to the bathroom. A moment later she joined him at the table where he'd set out their food. "Thank you for picking up dinner."

They ate in silence, Sierra amused by Beau's intense interest in the cooking show. "You can change the channel, if you'd like."

"Doesn't matter to me." He crushed his hamburger wrapper into a tiny ball and tossed it inside the food bag before digging into his fries.

Finished with her meal, Sierra escaped to the bathroom to brush her teeth. When she came out, Beau was sitting on the end of the bed. "My turn?" he asked.

"It's all yours."

After the bathroom door shut, Sierra climbed into bed and turned down the volume on the TV, preferring to listen to the sound of the shower and fantasize about Beau's naked, wet body. For someone who wasn't planning on any hanky-panky tonight she was torturing herself with X-rated images. She pulled the blanket higher as if it would smother the smoldering desire building in her body. To make love with Beau or not…Sierra was debating the issue when he stepped from the bathroom wearing a skimpy towel around his waist.

"You okay?" He stopped next to the bed. "You're turning blue."

Sierra gasped, unaware she'd been holding her breath. Good Lord, Beau's naked chest was all muscle that rippled when he moved his arms. Her gaze followed the line of hair that ran down the middle of his chest and disappeared beneath the edge of the terry cloth. Her eyes drifted lower, skimming over the body part she knew from experience was as impressive as his chest.

Then he turned away and she hissed when she noticed the red-and-purple welt above his hip. "What happened?" She gently brushed her fingers over the swollen mark.

"The bull's hoof caught me."

"Shouldn't you see a doctor?"

"It's just a bruise."

His answer rubbed her the wrong way. "So you can tell me what I should and shouldn't do, but when someone gives you advice you discount it and do what you want?"

He frowned.

Sierra got to her knees on the bed and pointed her finger. "You might as well get it off your chest."

"I don't know what you're talking about."

"You disapproved of me drag racing today."

The muscle along his jaw bunched but Beau held his tongue and that ignited Sierra's anger. "You think you know what's best for everyone but—"

"I don't take stupid chances."

"I wasn't taking a stupid chance. People drag race all the time and I had an instructor. I followed the rules and—"

"Ran the damned car off the track." He shoved a hand through his hair. "You could have been seriously injured."

She scoffed. "I hit a pile of rubber, and I wore a helmet and a safety harness."

"The car could have flipped over."

She sprang from the bed and paced across the carpet. "You're making a big deal out of it."

"And you're not making a big enough deal out of nothing."

A glare-down ensued. "You make me so mad I want to pull my hair out," she said.

"You make me so mad I want to kiss you."

They shouldn't. Not when they were angry. Not ever. Beau's towel slipped lower on his hips and Sierra sucked in a quiet breath.

Make love with Beau. She winced at the voice in her head. *You both want it.*

There was no mistaking the desire flashing in Beau's eyes.

It doesn't have to mean anything.

Her frustration with Beau taunted her to see how far she could push him, as if the exercise was sensual foreplay. "You owe me an apology," she said.

He crowded her space, his clean scent going to her head. "If anyone should apologize, it's you for making people worry."

"I didn't ask you to worry about me."

"Too bad. I can't help it."

They stood toe-to-toe, his hot stare breaking through her defenses. "And I can't help this." She curled her hand around his neck and brought his mouth to hers. The kiss was hot and wet and wild. Her fingers dipped beneath the edge of the terry cloth and gently caressed his injured hip. She thought she heard Beau groan as she loosened the knot at the front of the towel. Bingo! The covering fell to the floor.

No turning back now.

"You look damned sexy in my shirt." He nibbled her neck.

"And you," she whispered. "Look sexy wearing nothing."

He released the top snap of the shirt and kissed her exposed flesh…popped open the next snap…another kiss…on and on until he set her whole body on fire.

"Leave the light on, Beau." This would be the final

time they made love and Sierra wanted to experience every detail. One day she wouldn't be able to see Beau at all, so tonight she'd use all her other senses to commit him to memory. His taste…texture…scent…the sound of his breathing…then, when her eyes saw nothing but darkness, she'd recall this moment with Beau and remember it in vivid color.

Beau didn't care if they made love in the dark or bright sunlight. He didn't need to see Sierra's face to know she yearned for his touch. Her short gasp when he cupped her breast told him that she loved his hands on her. She curled a leg over the back of his thigh, aligning their bodies intimately and he groaned in her ear then sifted his fingers through her hair, messing the silky strands. He buried his nose in the scented cloud and walked her backward to the bed. "You smell incredible."

Her nails scraped his thigh, the tickling sensation intensifying his arousal. Her touch electrified his skin and he burned for her. Forget slow and easy.

They tumbled to the bed in a no-holds-barred race to the finish line.

THE REPETITIVE CLICKING sound coming from the room heater pushed its way into Beau's subconscious and he slowly awakened. His arms automatically tightened around the warm, naked body snuggled against his side. *Sierra*.

He smiled in the darkness. He and Sierra should argue more often if their spats ended in lovemaking. He found it incredibly sexy that she was a hellion in the bedroom and prim and proper in public—every man's fantasy wife.

Wife.

Wife meant marriage. Marriage meant a lifetime commitment.

He cared for Sierra a great deal and admitted his heart was heading full-steam ahead toward a deeper, lasting emotion. There was much he admired about her—the strength and courage she'd shown in the face of her parents' deaths. Moving her life to Roundup and starting a business. And what man wouldn't admire a woman with phenomenal cooking skills?

Beau even admitted—reluctantly—that he respected Sierra's stubborn pride. Yet, if he was honest with himself, he'd admit that being with Sierra scared him. Pressure built inside his chest, making it difficult to draw a deep breath. He didn't want to have this conversation with himself, but the voice in his head insisted.

Sierra's going blind.

That didn't change the way he felt about her.

How will you feel ten or twenty years from now, when Sierra needs a seeing-eye dog and she can no longer drive or manage the diner?

Beau yearned to believe he'd adjust to her needs as the eye disease progressed.

What if you don't?

His chest ached when he considered how worried he'd been after his father had informed him that Jordan had been unable to contact Sierra. If he thought she was vulnerable now... Beau pressed his lips together, picturing a future with him hovering and Sierra frustrated by the boundaries he'd insist on setting for her—for his own sanity. And what about the times he couldn't be with her...couldn't warn her of impending danger?

He thought about his goal to win an NFR title. How would he handle being on the road and not knowing what Sierra was doing or if she'd gotten herself into a situation where she needed help? Rodeo took every ounce of concentration he possessed. Would concern about Sierra's safety lurk in the far reaches of his mind each time he climbed onto the back of a bull?

Would his constant worry wear them down and ruin their relationship? He didn't want Sierra waking up one morning and resenting him and the stranglehold he had on her.

Don't forget children.

What about his desire to be a father? Did Sierra want children, knowing she'd be blind one day? Beau thought of his brother, Duke, and his cousins who were starting families of their own. He didn't want to be left out of the experience. If he persuaded Sierra to have children, was *he* up to the challenge of taking on the child-rearing responsibilities she couldn't manage on her own?

He pondered the amount of time and energy parents invested in caring for their children. How would he manage if he had to help out more than most fathers?

"Beau...?" Sierra's lips brushed against his neck and he shivered.

"Shh..." He didn't know who he'd shushed—the pessimistic voice in his head or Sierra.

"You're squeezing me too hard."

"Sorry." Beau relaxed his hold.

Like a gentle breeze, her sigh floated past his ear, the sound blowing away his negative thoughts, leaving only a raw desire to make love to her again. He rolled Sierra beneath him and kissed her, not caring if she tasted his desperation. He lost himself in her scent, feel and taste, each kiss and caress marking her as his, as he sought reassurance where there was none.

IN THE AFTERMATH of their lovemaking, Sierra listened to Beau's breathing transition from ragged to even and

knew the moment he'd fallen asleep—the heavy weight
of his arm relaxed across her chest, constricting her
breathing. Carefully she moved his arm aside, slipped
from the bed and retreated to the bathroom. After wrapping a towel around herself she sat on the edge of the
tub and rested her face in her hands.

Was she crazy?

Don't answer that.

Why couldn't she have been stronger and resisted
Beau? Now he was likely to believe he'd earned the right
to tell her what to do and interfere in her life.

There would never be a better time in her life for ex-
ploring the things she'd always dreamed of doing, but
Beau was like a big, tall boulder standing in her way.

As FAR AS morning-afters went, Sierra and Beau's wasn't
a big deal—at least that's the attitude *she* tried to convey. Sierra used the bathroom first, then watched the
local news while Beau finished dressing. When he
emerged from the bathroom, she said, "Sunny skies for
the next few days and the roads are clear." She checked
the time on her cell phone. "If we hurry, I can make it
back to Roundup by nine."

"While you were in the bathroom earlier, my father called and invited us out to the ranch for brunch,"
Beau said.

"That was nice of him, but I have to get to the diner."
Sierra didn't care to explain to anyone her spur-of-the-
moment decision to drag race.

"Jordan made arrangements for Irene to work the
whole day." Beau brushed a strand of hair from Sierra's
cheek, his finger lingering against her skin, stirring her
arousal. "We can spend the afternoon together," he said.

Sierra didn't want to take advantage of Irene, especially when she'd need her employee's loyalty in the future when Sierra's vision worsened. She cringed as she pictured herself struggling to find her way around the kitchen, experiment with new recipes and keep tabs on the diner's finances.

"I can't take the day off, Beau. I'll phone my aunt on the way to Roundup and let her know I won't be coming." The disappointment on Beau's face almost made Sierra change her mind.

He caressed her cheek, tilting her chin upward, then he kissed the sensitive patch of skin below her ear.

Knowing it wouldn't take much effort on his part to make her change her mind, Sierra said, "Beau, stop." She moved out of reach. "We can't... I'm not going to let... It's just that..." The emotions she'd tried to ignore when she'd woken this morning got the best of her and tears blurred her vision.

"What's wrong, honey?" He squeezed her shoulders.

"I can't think with you touching me." Sierra retreated to the other side of the room.

"That's a good thing, isn't it?" Beau's mouth curved in a sexy grin.

She didn't know where to begin, but she'd better figure it out quick or things would get out of hand and they'd end up back in bed. "We can't keep doing this."

"Doing what?"

"Having sex. We're just friends, remember?"

"I think we're more than friends, Sierra."

"No, last night was a mistake."

He jerked as if she'd slapped him. *Blast it*. This wasn't going well.

"What we shared was special."

"Be that as it may, my future is already mapped out for me, Beau."

"You enjoy being with me."

"Of course I've enjoyed your company." And making love…that had been off-the-charts enjoyable.

In two strides he gathered her in his arms. "What's got you running scared?"

It would be so easy to take a chance on Beau, but for her own survival she had to face the future alone. "In case you've forgotten, I'm going blind."

"Not for a long time."

She pressed her hands against Beau's chest, forcing a little space between them. Was he being obtuse on purpose or did he really view the two of them riding into the sunset together and living happily ever after? If so, then she had to protect him as well as herself.

"You're going to run away from what we have— could have—because you're afraid," Beau said.

"If you aren't afraid of a future with me then you sure as heck should be." She grabbed her coat and purse and fled the room.

The ride back to the Yellowstone Drag Strip was made in stony silence and not until Sierra got into her own car did she breathe a sigh of relief. Of course, for the entire drive to Roundup the headlights of Beau's truck shone in the rearview mirror.

When they reached the outskirts of town, Beau took the turnoff to Thunder Ranch. Sierra drove the rest of the way to the diner, ignoring the pain in her heart as she contemplated what next to tackle on her bucket list.

Chapter Twelve

Beau parked in front of his father's house and a moment later the front door opened. Joshua Adams stepped outside, Jordan right behind him.

"You made good time." Joshua stared at Beau's truck.

"Sierra's not coming," Beau said.

Jordan frowned. "Where is she?"

Sierra hadn't phoned her aunt? "Sierra said she needed to get back to the diner."

"But I phoned Irene and she—"

"I told Sierra, but she didn't want to impose on Irene." Beau silently cursed. Why was he making excuses for Sierra?

"Would you mind if I have a word with Beau, Jordan?"

"Of course not." Jordan went inside the house and shut the door.

Beau wasn't in the mood for a lecture and the look on his father's face warned he was in for one.

"What happened between you and Sierra that made her not want to be here this morning?"

"Do we have to get into this right now?" Beau was tired and frustrated. Sierra had put him through the ringer the past eighteen hours.

"You better not have crossed the line in that motel room last night."

That's it. Beau had had enough. "And what if I did?"

His father's face reddened. "I warned you—"

"Lay off, Dad. You were a crappy father to Duke and me when we were kids. You haven't earned the right to tell me what to do with my personal life. And just because you have feelings for Jordan doesn't mean your relationship with her is more important than mine with Sierra. It's your problem if you can't live with that." Beau walked off to the barn.

"Where are you going? Your brother and Angie will be here any minute."

"I'm not hungry. Eat without me." Beau went straight into his workshop. He had a few finishing touches to put on the Phillips saddle. Depending on how long he remained angry with his father, Phillips might get some fancy stitching in the leather that he hadn't asked for.

Less than an hour had passed when Duke appeared in the doorway. "I suppose Dad sent you out here," Beau said.

His brother didn't deny the charge. Duke nodded to the saddle stand in the corner. "Is that one finished?"

"Almost. I'm working on the toe fenders." Beau motioned to the bench where various strips of leather lay.

Duke examined the intricate stitching along the seat. "Pretty fancy for a work saddle."

"You didn't come out here to discuss my leather-working skills, did you?"

His even-tempered twin didn't rise to the bait. "I remember the belts and wrist bands you made in middle school. You've come a long way from those days."

"I have you to thank for telling me I was nuts not to make money off my hobby."

"You repaid me when you made a saddle for my eighteenth birthday," Duke said.

"Keeping that a secret was tough."

"Is that why you put a lock on your workshop door?" Duke asked.

"Heck, yes." Beau dabbed a cloth in linseed oil then polished a toe fender.

"You used to come out here when Dad was in a bad mood," Duke said.

"And you'd lock yourself in your bedroom and watch Westerns." Beau set the cloth aside.

"Is everything okay between you and Sierra?" Duke had finally stopped beating around the bush.

"We're fine." They weren't, but damned if Beau would discuss his troubled love life with his brother.

"Dad wants you to back off for a while and allow Sierra a chance to come to grips with the reality of her situation," Duke said.

The last thing Sierra needed was to be left alone. Look at the trouble she'd already gotten into—drinking too much and drag racing. The risks she'd taken sent his blood pressure skyrocketing.

"Angie and Jordan put a plate of leftovers in the fridge for you." Duke checked his watch. "I'm on duty this afternoon." He paused at the door. "Just a heads-up…Dad and Jordan are going to the movies later and he wants you to move the bulls to the north pasture."

"Figures."

"I could call Dinah. Maybe she can cover for me while I help you," Duke said.

"I'll be fine. Thanks, though."

After Duke left, Beau flung the oil rag across the

room. He didn't want to give Sierra more space, but he didn't have much of a choice.

Space or no space, he and Sierra weren't through yet.

SIERRA WAITED UNTIL the last possible moment before turning out the diner lights and heading up to her apartment. She'd managed to avoid her aunt all day but knew an inquisition awaited her. "It's just me," she said when she entered the living room. Her voice woke Jordan who'd fallen asleep on the couch with a book in her hands.

"What time is it?"

"Ten-thirty," Sierra answered.

"You're closing up awfully late tonight."

"I did a little extra cleaning."

"Sit down." Jordan patted the sofa cushion next to her.

Sierra obeyed. "How are things between you and Joshua?"

Her aunt's cheeks turned pink. "I stayed the night at the ranch with him."

She and Beau had been…while Jordan and Joshua had been… *Don't go there.* "I'm happy you and Joshua are getting along so well."

"It's deeper than that, dear."

"You mean you might move here permanently?" That would be one worry off Sierra's mind, knowing her aunt was close by to help her through the tough times ahead.

"I'm fifty-eight years old and I'm not getting any younger. I want a second chance with Joshua, but first I need to make sure you're okay."

"What do you mean? I'm fine."

"I have no doubt you will be fine, but right now you're running scared."

Sierra opened her mouth to protest but nothing came out. Okay, so she was frightened of going blind. Most people would be, but that didn't mean she was running from anything.

"You didn't tell anyone where you were went yesterday."

Guilty.

"Beau said I should ask you what you were doing in Billings."

"I'm an adult, Aunt Jordan. I didn't think I had to check in with you or my employees."

"That may be, but it was inconsiderate not to inform someone of your whereabouts. What if I'd gotten ill? Joshua wouldn't have been able to reach you."

Guilt pricked Sierra. "Just because my eyesight isn't the greatest doesn't mean I have to give up my privacy and let everyone know my business."

"I understand how you're feeling right now. You want to believe the test results were wrong and you're praying the disease will somehow cure itself."

Yes, Sierra was struggling to accept her fate but deep down she felt time was running out and every minute that passed was a minute she couldn't gain back before she went blind. No one was going to stop her from living each day to the fullest. "Aunt Jordan…"

"Yes, dear."

"What did you do after the doctor told you that you'd eventually lose your sight?"

"I cried for twenty-four hours straight. Poor Bob didn't know what to do with me."

"After the tears…what then?"

"A sense of urgency took over inside me. The first week I remained awake almost twenty-four hours a day, worried I'd miss something exciting if I went to sleep."

Bingo! That's exactly how Sierra felt. "Did that feeling pass?"

"Eventually. Your uncle insisted I needed something to focus on other than my deteriorating eyesight so he told me to get a job."

"A job?" That wasn't the answer Sierra had expected.

"Bob said I had to be able to take care of myself as I grew older, especially if I outlived him, which happened to be the case. And he was protecting his own interests."

"How so?"

"He didn't want my blindness to prevent him from doing the things he'd always enjoyed in life, like taking a yearly fishing trip to Canada with his buddies. He knew he couldn't travel if he had to worry about leaving me alone at home."

"You make adjusting to your blindness sound easy."

"Easy?" Jordan laughed. "I was terrified. And the worst part was that I couldn't show Bob how scared I was or he'd have slacked off on his tough love, and the progress I'd made would have been for nothing." Jordan reached for Sierra's hand. "I wish I'd had someone to confide in. Someone who'd gone through what I was going through. Someone to tell me that it would be okay. That I'd be okay."

Sierra wished she could ask Beau to stand by her side and help her, but she refused to be a burden to him. "I don't know what I'm going to do if I have to sell the diner," Sierra whispered. Cooking was her life's blood. If she was forced to give up her sight so be it, but not being able to cook…that would be devastating.

"Why would you have to sell the diner?" her aunt asked.

"How would I know if one of the employees took money from the cash register? Or stole food from the pantry? They could rob me blind—no pun intended—and I wouldn't know."

"Then don't allow yourself to be taken advantage of. Memorize every inch of your kitchen and pantry and rely on your friends to help watch over your employees."

"It seems...overwhelming."

"Running the diner will allow you to lead a fulfilling life. Even when you can't see the food you prepare, you'll be able to taste it. You'll find that when you lose your sight, your sense of smell and taste will improve and that might even make you a better chef."

Sierra drew strength from her aunt's reassurances. Nothing would weaken the blow of living in darkness, but working in the diner would give her a sense of purpose and a place to be every day—better to fumble around the kitchen than to sit in her apartment and feel sorry for herself. "I'm going to miss seeing the golden color of a perfectly baked pie crust and the soft pink tinge of my almond-raspberry frosting."

And Beau's beautiful brown eyes.

"Never underestimate the power of your memory. Your mind will recall all your favorite things in brilliant color."

As her aunt's words soaked in, Sierra decided that once she tackled her bucket list she'd settle down and plan for her future. With her aunt's help she was determined to keep the Number 1 Diner the most popular restaurant in town.

WEDNESDAY MORNING SIERRA entered the diner kitchen and set her backpack by the door. Before she'd taken a step toward the coffeepot, her cell phone went off. She checked the number. Beau. *Again.*

Since she and Beau had returned from Billings on

Sunday, he'd left her numerous voice mail messages. He claimed he was calling to make sure she was okay. Okay from what? Their lovemaking? The drag race? Their argument before leaving the motel? She understood her actions worried Beau and that he wanted her promise she wouldn't go off and do something crazy, but right now the only person she was making promises to was herself. As a matter of fact, Beau's overprotectiveness had pushed Sierra to schedule her next adventure sooner rather than later, before he or anyone else changed her mind.

Sierra filled her thermos with coffee, grabbed her backpack and almost made it out the door before Irene waltzed into the kitchen. Darn. Sierra had been hoping to escape the diner without having to answer any questions.

"Will you be back before eight or should I close up tonight?" Irene asked.

"I'll be back." If she wasn't, that meant she was stuck sleeping in her car in the mountains.

"Have fun...wherever you're off to."

"Thanks, Irene." Sierra slipped outside, got into her car and drove toward the Bull Mountains where she planned to meet up with a bungee-jumping group and take her first and only leap off the railroad trestle bridge that spanned Sweetwater Canyon. The drive would take a half hour, and then the group would hike another twenty minutes to the bridge. Sierra's blood pumped faster as she imagined free-falling three-hundred feet— the length of a football field.

After today's jump, the remaining items on her bucket list weren't as exciting—a cruise, a shopping spree along Rodeo Drive, a Broadway play, a trip to Europe, and she wanted to visit Egypt.

When Sierra parked at the ranger's station she searched her backpack for her bucket list so she could cross off bungee jumping, but it was nowhere to be found. She must have left it in the pocket of her other coat—the one she'd worn Sunday to the racetrack. Backpack in hand, Sierra introduced herself to the other jumpers.

By the time the group reached the trestle bridge, Sierra was huffing and puffing. Their leader, Scott, attached the gear to the bridge then checked the safety equipment. Sierra chatted with Lisa, a twenty-two-year-old graduate student from Montana State University who was visiting family in the area. She and her boyfriend, Alan, had planned this jump to celebrate their recent engagement. Sierra would have loved to invite Beau along today, but he'd have insisted the jump was too risky.

Once the equipment was ready, Scott asked if Sierra would like to jump first and she agreed. He helped her into the body harness, which served as a backup to the ankle attachment, then he checked the length of the braided shock cord, explaining that it needed to be significantly shorter than the three-hundred-foot drop to allow the elastic to stretch. Once Sierra was ready, Scott assisted her over the bridge rail to a small platform that extended away from the structure. Sierra refused to glance down, instead she looked straight ahead at the beautiful pine-covered butte at the far end of the canyon.

"Whenever you're ready, Sierra," Scott said.

"I'll take plenty of pictures." Alan's hobby was photography and he'd offered to snap photos of Sierra's jump.

One...two...three! Sierra launched herself into the air. The rush of the cold wind hitting her face snatched her breath as everything around became a blur. She'd been falling forever when the rope snapped her backward toward the top of the bridge—the going up almost as much fun as the going down.

When Sierra's rebound leveled off, she felt a hard jerk and the body harness tightened around her chest with crushing force. For a few terrifying seconds she twirled in a circle, then hung suspended over the dry riverbed filled with large boulders and jagged rocks. Her heart pounded with fear and her mind raced with horrifying images of the rope snapping sending her spiraling to her death. She resisted glancing over her shoulder, fearing any unnecessary movement might sever the cord.

"Don't move, Sierra! Help is on the way!"

Her fate in the hands of others, Sierra dangled over the bridge, wishing she'd told Beau that, even though they couldn't be together, she loved him.

"You SITTING DOWN?" Duke asked when Beau answered his cell phone.

Beau had just finished loading hay onto the flatbed and was heading out to fill the bale feeders in the pasture. "Sitting down—fat chance." He wiped his sweaty brow with the sleeve of his flannel shirt. "I'm working my ass off. Dad's at home showering for his date with Jordan tonight. What's going on?"

"It's Sierra."

Beau's heart gave a tiny lurch. Sierra had ignored his phone calls the past few days and although he didn't want to admit it, he was hurt. "What's she gone and done now?"

"I'm on my way up to the Bull Mountains. We got an emergency call from the park ranger. A bungee jumper got their gear caught on the old Johnston Railroad Trestle Bridge."

Beau swallowed hard as he walked quickly to his truck. He knew in gut without even asking. "It's Sierra."

"'Fraid so. You heading up there?"

"I'm on my way." Cussing up a storm, Beau peeled out of the driveway. Once he turned onto the highway he dialed his father's cell and left a message. He tried hard not to think about Sierra hanging precariously off a bridge. What the hell was she thinking—bungee jumping? She wasn't a daredevil. She was a woman who spent her days cooking in the kitchen.

By the time he arrived in the parking area at the head of the trail leading to the bridge, his muscles were tied in knots. He spotted Sierra's car and several other vehicles, as well as Duke's patrol unit. It was the fire-and-rescue truck that sent a cold chill down his spine. Making sure he had his phone, Beau entered the path. He'd never walked so fast in his life, and when he arrived on the scene he almost had a heart attack. Sierra dangled at least two hundred feet over the side of the bridge. Her head drooped forward and Beau feared she'd passed out. As he approached the group, he listened to the forest ranger speak.

"We're going to drop another rope down to Sierra and she's got to attach it to the harness. There's a small metal ring on the front where the clip can be secured."

The forest ranger pulled out a bullhorn and shouted instructions to Sierra, asking her to raise her hand if she understood him. Sierra lifted her arm only a few inches. Beau prayed to God she didn't pass out before she attached the rescue rope to the body harness.

The forest ranger tossed the rope over the bridge away from Sierra, then guided the rope closer until it bumped her body. No one said a word as they watched and waited for Sierra to grasp the rope. After two attempts she held the end.

"What's wrong?" Beau asked the park ranger when Sierra fumbled with the self-locking hook.

"She might be having trouble finding the ring. It's small." The ranger shouted encouragement but just when she located the ring, the safety rope slipped from her hand.

Beau was sweating profusely as Duke stood at his side. The park ranger once again wiggled the rope close to Sierra and this time she succeeded in attaching the clip to the ring. The forest ranger and the bungee-jumping instructor slowly hoisted her up—the longest minute of Beau's life. When they lifted her over the rail he rushed forward but was blocked by the paramedics who began taking Sierra's vitals.

Duke clamped a hand around Beau's arm and he was grateful for the bruising hold. He'd rather square off with a bull any day than suffer the overwhelming helplessness he felt right now as he watched the paramedics work on Sierra.

"Is she going to be okay?" he asked. No one answered. Unable to stand back and watch any longer he broke free of Duke's hold and squeezed between the two paramedics. "Sierra, its Beau." He knelt by her head. "Can you hear me, honey?" When her eyes remained closed, he leaned down and whispered, "You're going to be okay. Hang in there." She had to be fine—he refused to believe anything else.

The hike down the mountain with Sierra on a stretcher was long and arduous. When they reached the trailhead, Duke spoke to the paramedics. "I'll give you guys an escort." Before Duke climbed into his patrol car, he said, "I'll call Dad and let him know where they're taking Sierra. Meet you at the hospital." Duke flipped on the emergency lights and led the way out of the park. After the rescue truck left, the park ranger packed up his gear and drove off. The bungee-jumping instructor looked like he needed a drink and offered to buy the young couple a round at the Open Range Saloon. Beau imagined news of Sierra's mishap would spread like wildfire if it hadn't already.

Once the parking lot cleared and Beau was left alone, he walked into the bushes and heaved until his stomach was empty. Feeling shaky, he took a bottle of water from the cooler he kept in the backseat. Sticking out from beneath the cooler on the floor was a sheet of notebook paper that didn't belong to him. He tugged the paper free.

Sierra's Bucket List had been printed across the top. Beau read the items listed on the paper.

#1 Drag Race

#2 Bungee Jumping

#3 Vacation in Egypt

#4 Shop on Rodeo Drive

Beau skimmed the rest of the items, ticked off that *he* wasn't on the list. If Sierra was taking risks, why wasn't she willing to trust him and give their relationship a chance? He crumpled the paper in his fist. Sierra could have died today—all because of a stupid bucket list. He shoved the wad of paper into his pocket and started the truck.

The drive out of the park took forever and by the time Beau arrived at the hospital, a crowd had gathered in the emergency room. He waved Duke down. "How's Sierra?"

"She's got some bruising where the harness bit into

her chest, and they're keeping her overnight for observation, but the risk of a blood clot is minimal. She was lucky, Beau. The doctor said he's seen people die after being suspended in the air thirty minutes or less."

"Does Jordan know?"

"Yeah. Dad's on his way over here with her. If you want any privacy with Sierra, you'd better talk to her now." Duke pointed to the curtained-off cubical at the end of the corridor.

Beau walked down the hall, and cleared his throat before moving the curtain aside. Sierra slowly opened her eyes. When she saw him, she attempted to smile, but her effort was weak at best. He pulled a chair next to the bed and sat. They stared at each other for a long time, then tears trickled from her eyes. Beau's throat tightened as he struggled to get a grip on his emotions. After a minute he pulled the crumpled note from his pocket and handed it to Sierra. "I believe this belongs to you."

"I thought I'd lost it," she whispered, wiping her tears with the edge of the sheet.

"Why?" Beau asked.

"Why what?"

"Why are you so hell-bent on taking chances and putting yourself in danger?"

"You wouldn't understand," she said.

"Try me."

"When the doctor said I'd eventually go blind, I thought about all the things I'd dreamed of doing one day."

"So why am I not on your list?" he asked.

Her eyes widened before she dropped her gaze to her lap. "Don't, Beau."

"Don't what?"

"Don't pretend there's any future for us."

Her words sucker punched Beau. After all they'd been through together, Sierra refused to admit that what they'd shared had been more than just a good time. He had to get out of there before he exploded and said something he could never take back. Beau fled the cubical but paused in the hallway, waiting…hoping…she'd call him back.

She didn't.

Chapter Thirteen

"Have you called Ace?" Duke asked his cousin Colt when he arrived at his aunt's house.

"Yeah. Thought he ought to see this."

Duke leaned against the grille of Colt's truck and watched his twin go head-to-head with Midnight in the corral.

"Mom saw him take a nasty fall a half hour ago and told him to quit."

"He ignored her," Duke said.

"Yeah, so she called me because—"

"Ace would have a fit."

Colt grinned. "Sheesh, hoss. You'd think *we* were twins the way you finish my thoughts."

Duke wanted to intervene but knew his brother would object. "Midnight's not tiring, is he?"

"Nope."

A horn blast caught their attention. Ace's pickup barreled into the ranch yard. When he got out of the truck, he hollered, "What's so all-fired important that I had to drive—" Ace stopped in his tracks and stared at Beau picking himself up off the ground.

"You didn't tell Ace that Beau was riding Midnight?" Duke whispered.

"Nope."

"What the hell's he doing?" Ace joined his brother and cousin.

"Mom gave Beau the go-ahead to get Midnight ready for the rodeo in South Dakota," Colt said.

"Nice of Mom to tell me," Ace grumbled.

"She said you had enough on your plate with work and Flynn getting ready to have the baby."

All three men winced when Beau stumbled on the way back to the chute and did a face-plant in the dirt. He crawled to his knees, then his feet and staggered forward.

"For God's sake, it looks like he broke his nose," Ace said. Blood dripped off Beau's chin, but he wiped it away with his shirtsleeve.

"Why's he beating himself up?" Ace directed the question to Duke.

"It's Sierra." The look in Beau's eyes when he saw Sierra dangling from the bridge would haunt Duke for a long time. He'd never seen his brother so scared. There was no doubt in Duke's mind that Beau was in love with Sierra.

"I heard about her close call," Ace said.

Duke cleared his throat. "Shook Beau up pretty bad."

"Didn't know Beau and Sierra were a couple. Then again, I'm so dang busy with my practice I don't know much about what goes on in this family anymore."

"Leah said Flynn called her after talking to Dinah, who'd run into Cheyenne at the diner, who'd heard from Jordan that Sierra had made out a bucket list and bungee jumping was on it," Colt said.

Ace stared at his brother as if he'd grown two heads. "I'm supposed to make sense out of what you just said?"

Duke clarified things. "Ever since Sierra found out she inherited her aunt's eye disease, and will probably end up blind one day, she's been participating in extreme activities like bungee jumping and drag racing."

Ace whistled low. "Let me guess, Beau's trying to stop her and she's telling him to get out of her way."

"That sums it up pretty well," Duke said.

Colt pointed to the pen. "Watch this, Ace. Midnight backs himself into position." The stallion spun then inched into the makeshift chute.

"If that don't beat all," Ace whispered.

Beau attempted to climb the rails, his boot slipping on the rungs.

"How long has he been at it?" Ace asked.

"Not sure. At least an hour, I'd guess," Colt said.

Once he'd climbed onto Midnight's back, Beau lifted the hay rake and clanged it against the metal rail. The horse bolted into the pen and Beau dropped the rake. "Midnight's hardly winded and he's still bucking high and tight," Colt said.

All three men let out a whoop when the stallion leapt into the air as he bucked. "He's a high-roller," Ace said.

Beau went flying.

"C'mon, Ace." Colt nudged his brother's arm. "Admit it. Midnight was born to rodeo."

"There's no denying the horse loves to buck." Ace shook his head. "Midnight's already in the chute and Beau hasn't even gotten to his feet."

"Beau's had enough." Duke made a move toward the pen where his twin lay spread-eagle in the dirt.

"Wait." Ace snagged his cousin's jacket.

"Beau's riding in the Miles City Rodeo this Saturday. If he keeps this up he'll be in no shape to compete," Duke said.

"I'll talk to him." Ace took two steps then stopped and pinned Colt with a glare. "You wouldn't by chance be thinking of entering Midnight in the Miles City Rodeo, would you?" Colt remained silent. "There's no sense taking a chance he'll injure himself before the Bash." When Colt remained mute, Ace grumbled and marched off.

"You're taking Midnight, aren't you?" Duke asked. "Never mind. I don't want to know."

Beau saw his older cousin heading his way. Ace didn't look pleased. Dragging his sore butt off the ground, Beau ignored the man and limped toward the chute where Midnight waited for him.

"Haven't you had enough punishment for one day?" Ace slipped through the rails of the pen and cut across the dirt.

"Butt out, Ace." Beau stepped on the lower rung and a sharp twinge shot through his ankle. He lost his balance and Ace's hand shot out to steady him.

"Come on, look at yourself. Your nose is bleeding. You've got a split lip. You better…" Ace let his words trail off.

"I better what?"

"Stick to bulls. You suck at bronc busting."

"Think you can do better?"

"Hell, yes, I can ride better than you, but—"

"Chicken shit," Beau mumbled.

"What'd you call me?" Ace shoved Beau into the rails.

"Chicken shit!" Beau's shout propelled his brother and Colt across the drive and into the pen.

"What's going on?" Colt stepped between Beau and Ace.

"Get out of my way." Ace climbed the rails and straddled Midnight. "How do I get him to leave the chute?"

Without warning Beau clanged the rake against the

rail. The noise sent Midnight into action and Ace almost got tossed on his head. He managed to keep his seat, but his hat flew off as the stallion did its best to throw his rider.

Colt and Duke hollered encouragement. Beau stood silent—glaring. Eventually Midnight decided he'd had enough and launched Ace into the air. Beau's cousin landed with a loud *oomph* but got to his feet smiling.

"Whoo-wee, Ace!" Colt hollered. "I thought you we're going to ride the buck out of Midnight."

The stallion trotted past Ace then stopped in front of Beau as if waiting for him to concede defeat. "You win." Beau patted Midnight's neck.

"I'll walk him to the barn." Ace removed the bucking strap and bareback rope from Midnight and handed them to Beau before leading the stallion away. "C'mon, Midnight. You've earned a rubdown." Colt followed his brother, leaving Duke and Beau facing off.

"What?" Beau said when Duke watched him in silence. "Don't you have criminals to chase after?"

"I'm going to give you a pass for being a jerk. You know why?"

"I don't care why, but—" Beau spat at the ground "—you'll tell me anyway."

"You're pissed off because Sierra doesn't want anything to do with you."

"Butt out, Duke."

"Instead of beating yourself up, why don't you see if you can make nice with her?"

"And tell her what? I don't care that she's going blind?" His outburst startled Duke. "Well, I do care! I frickin' care that the woman I love—" Startled by the pronouncement, Beau lost his train of thought.

Love. Worried about Sierra's eye disease and the impact it would have on their relationship…his rodeo future…having children… Beau had refused to say the word out loud or even think it until just now. The feeling had been inside him for a while, but the fear of her waking up one day in the dark and him unable to prevent it had him running scared.

"You ever consider Sierra might not believe it's her you're in love with?" Duke asked.

"What the hell's that supposed to mean?"

"Are you sure the love you feel for Sierra isn't grounded in your need to protect her and be the one she leans on for help? You have a habit of making people depend on you, Beau. Look how long it took me to stand up to you."

"This is none of your business."

"Actually, I believe it is my business, seeing how I was a victim of your overprotectiveness most of my life."

Victim? Beau was speechless—good thing, since his brother had plenty to say.

"You've always looked out for me, Beau."

Wasn't that good?

"When Dad left me to fend for myself against the bullies on the playground, I was grateful you stood up for me."

"But…"

"You don't know when to back off." Duke shoved his hands into the pockets of his jeans. "You know what hurts the most?"

Beau waited for his brother to tell him.

"You didn't believe in me."

"What the hell are you talking about?"

"You never believed I was good enough to win on my own. You felt you had to lose to help build my self-esteem. You never gave me the chance to prove to myself, or you, or anybody for that matter, that I was good enough to beat you when you were trying your hardest."

After giving his brother's words thought, Beau said, "What does this have to do with my feelings for Sierra?"

"You smother people, Beau. You step in and take over for others when they don't want your interference."

Bullshit. Duke didn't know what the hell he was talking about.

"You don't even realize what you're doing, but you make people dependent on you, then—"

"They resent me," Beau said.

"I don't resent you, but you should have allowed me to fail or succeed on my own."

Beau didn't say a word. His brother was on a roll and he sensed this discussion was far from over.

"Not until I met Angie did I realize I was riding for all the wrong reasons. Angie gave me the strength I needed to admit that, as much as I enjoyed busting bulls, I was winning for you, Beau—not me."

Beau's chest tightened, making it tough to draw a deep breath. "I'm sorry."

"I didn't bring this up because I want an apology, but because you're headed down the same path with Sierra."

Beau's stomach bottomed out. He thought back to the times he and Sierra had been together—had he been overprotective? Smothering? If he had, couldn't she see that it had been because he cared? "Sierra's going to be blind one day. She should realize that she'll need people to help her. She can't go through this alone."

"I get it now," Duke said.

"Get what?" Beau had trouble following the conversation.

"I get why you're upset."

Normally Beau was the one to hand out advice. That he took his brother's words into account confirmed how shaken up he was over Sierra.

"You can't handle the idea that Sierra doesn't need you the way you want her to need you."

"Of course she needs me."

"Think, Beau. We grew up without a mother and Dad wasn't all that affectionate. Aside from Aunt Sarah's hugs, we weren't raised in a warm, fuzzy home."

"So?"

"My insecurities played out in my stuttering and yours played out by being overprotective of me. You wanted me to depend on you so you'd always feel needed."

His brother had gone straight for the jugular. Beau stared into the distance, trying to make sense of Duke's words. Had he unconsciously made people depend on him because of a need for love and affection?

"Remember when I told you I was quitting rodeo? You freaked out."

Beau had flown into a rage, because he'd believed Duke hadn't appreciated all the sacrifices he'd made for his brother through the years. If there was any truth to Duke's words, Beau had been upset not because his brother had quit bull riding, but because he no longer needed Beau—Duke had found Angie.

Shit. He needed a frickin' therapist.

"I don't doubt for a minute you care deeply for Sierra, Beau. Just be sure your feelings are true blue and not tied to wanting her to depend on you."

Well, hell. Did Sierra believe he was more in love with the need to rescue her than just plain love her? But he did love Sierra, and when you loved someone it was only natural that you wanted to protect them. The two went hand in hand. "Leave me alone, Duke."

His brother walked off, but stopped a few feet away. "Beau."

"What?"

"I may not need you to lose rodeos for me or beat up bullies on the playground, but I do still need you to be my brother."

Beau struggled to draw air into his pinched lungs as he watched Duke get into his truck and drive away.

"SIERRA?"

Leave me be, Aunt Jordan.

"Sierra, dear? Where are you?" The sound of Jordan's low-heeled shoes clicking against the floor echoed above Sierra's head.

As was normal on a Friday night, the diner had been packed and she'd closed a half hour later than usual. Physically and emotionally exhausted, Sierra yearned for a hot soak in the tub, but halfway up the back stairs the memory of Beau's kiss in the darkened hallway had overwhelmed her and she'd given in to the tears she'd held at bay since the afternoon at the hospital when she'd hurt Beau's feelings.

"Sierra?" Before she summoned the energy to call out to her aunt, the door at the top of the stairs opened. "I know you're here somewhere."

"I'm sorry, Aunt Jordan. I just wanted time to…to—"

"To what, dear?" Her aunt descended the steps, stopping when the tip of her shoe bumped Sierra's shoulder. "Scoot over."

Sierra inched closer to the wall, making room for her aunt. She didn't want to burden Jordan with her broken heart, especially when her aunt's love life was moving along strong and steady, but Sierra felt like she'd explode if she didn't share her pain with someone.

"I'm in love with Beau, Aunt Jordan, and it hurts that we can't be together." The floodgates opened and tears dripped down her cheeks.

"Why can't you be together?"

Sierra swallowed an angry retort. Her aunt acted as if going blind was just a bump in the road, but Sierra's failing eyesight felt like a noose around her neck, slowly tightening and choking the life out of her. "I can't be with Beau because I'd be a burden to him."

And because he'd insist on doing everything for me. Instead of becoming independent, she'd become dependent on Beau and then if—when—he left her, she'd... Sierra couldn't imagine the pain.

"Are you implying then that I'm a burden to Joshua because I'm blind?"

Sierra had never heard her aunt raise her voice before. "No, I didn't mean—"

"Shame on you, Sierra. Just because you can't see, doesn't mean you can't lead a fulfilling life or that you should sit back and feel sorry for yourself as the years pass you by." Her aunt put her arm around Sierra's shoulder. "And don't you dare accuse me of oversimplifying the situation."

"But you make it sound as if it's easy to adjust to living in the dark."

"Sometimes one chooses to remember the good mostly and not so much the bad...self-preservation, I guess. But don't think for a minute that I've forgotten the hardship I faced and still do because I can't see." Her aunt brushed a thumb across Sierra's wet cheek. "I, too, cried my share of tears and experienced moments of sheer panic when I did something by myself for the first time—like riding the city bus alone."

"You've shown me that it's possible to be blind and remain independent but…"

"But what?"

"I'm scared."

"It's okay to be scared, Sierra. You wouldn't be human if you didn't fear the unknown, but that's why I'm here. And Beau will help you, too."

"I don't want to rely on Beau."

"He cares about you."

"It's because he cares that I can't be with him."

"That doesn't make sense, dear."

"Beau's a take-charge guy who jumps in and helps out without being asked."

"Some women would find that chivalrous."

"If I allow Beau to do everything for me, I won't learn how to get around on my own and then I'll become too dependent on him and one day he'll wake up and realize how exhausting it is to take care of me and he'll leave. And then where will I be…trying to manage my life after years of having someone do it for me."

"Talk to Beau. Tell him what you need and don't need from him."

If Sierra thought asking Beau to back off would be enough, she'd have said so weeks ago, but a person shouldn't have to change who they were to be with the one they loved. And that wasn't all she feared. "Beau deserves to be a father and I'm not having any children."

"Why not? You'd be a wonderful mother."

"Children are a huge responsibility and my blindness would put my children in jeopardy."

"There are no guarantees in life, Sierra, but you're

the type of woman who wouldn't take chances with her children and I know you'd be extra vigilant—"

"Which could be a bad thing, too, because then I'd smother my kids and they'd grow up to hate me for it." Good grief, with both her and Beau being overprotective parents, their children would run away at the first opportunity.

"Nothing worth having in life comes without risks."

Sierra understood that, but did she have the courage to put her heart in Beau's hands and trust that he was strong enough for both of them when the going got tough…tougher…toughest?

"MIND SOME COMPANY?"

Beau glanced up from the workbench in the barn where he'd been putting the final touches on the saddle for Jim Phillips. His father hovered in the doorway.

"I thought you and Jordan had a standing date on Friday nights." Beau pushed a stool forward and his father sat.

"Jordan called a little while ago and said she and Sierra are watching a movie tonight." His father studied Beau's face. "The cut on your lip looks better."

Beau appreciated that his father hadn't grilled him when he'd come into the house two days ago looking as if he'd been run over by a truck. He suspected Aunt Sarah had informed her brother about Beau's impromptu rodeo with Midnight.

"You still plan to compete tomorrow in Miles City?"

"Yep." His aches and bruises hadn't healed but he didn't care.

"You sure that's smart?"

Beau shrugged, positive it wasn't smart. But again, he just didn't give a damn.

"You know…" His father pretended interest in the scrap of leather Beau tossed aside. "Maybe I came down a little too hard on you about Sierra."

This was a first. His father admitting he'd been wrong must be Jordan's influence. Amazing how a woman could waltz into a man's life and shake it up so violently that when the dust settled there was a whole new man standing there.

"Jordan put you up to this, didn't she?" Beau set aside his swivel knife.

"She's worried about Sierra."

"Dad, I—"

His father held up his hand. "Before you say anything…what are your intentions toward Sierra?"

"Are you asking because she and I spent the night together in a motel room?"

"No. As you pointed out earlier, that's none of my business." His father stared thoughtfully. "When you look ahead through the years, do you picture yourself with Sierra?"

After giving the question serious consideration, Beau said, "I can't imagine not having her in my life."

"Jordan's talked to me about her experience going blind."

Beau wasn't in the mood to discuss Jordan but he kept his mouth shut.

"When Jordan was diagnosed with the disease she asked her husband if he was going to divorce her."

"What did he say?"

"He'd told her that he'd married her for better or worse and wouldn't abandon her. Jordan acknowledged that he got her through several rough patches."

How many rough patches would Sierra experience,

and how long would they last? When Beau imagined being by her side, he had no idea what that entailed.

"The thing is, Jordan had been with her husband several years and they had a strong marriage before she'd been diagnosed with the disease."

"I'm not following."

"Most newlyweds have no idea what the future holds for them, which is a good thing if any marriage is to have a shot at succeeding. God forbid, if I had known how things would have turned out for me and your mother…" His voice trailed off. After a moment, he said, "You and Sierra know exactly what you're up against. If you choose to make a commitment to her and years down the road you suddenly become tired of living with a blind person and want out…that's a lot more hurtful than walking away now."

The words were difficult to hear, but Beau appreciated his father's candor.

"According to Jordan, going blind is the scariest thing in the world. For the first time in her life she had to learn to trust. Not just trust her husband when he said there was one step in front of her, not two, but she had to trust that the stranger she asked to help her in the grocery store actually handed her the can of soup she'd requested and not something different. And she had to trust the man on the corner who said the light was green and it was safe for her to cross the street."

Beau put himself in Sierra's shoes and pictured what it would be like to rely on a stranger's word. Right now, Sierra could see the sincerity in Beau's eyes, but what about ten or twenty years from now when he said "I love you" and she couldn't see the truth of the words in his expression? Sierra would have to take an incredible leap of faith if she wanted to be with him.

His father got up from the stool and patted Beau's back. "It was selfish of me to warn you away from Sierra. I didn't want anyone or anything to ruin my chances with Jordan."

"Dad?" Beau called out when his father turned to leave. "Are you afraid to be with Jordan because she's blind?"

"No. As much as I wanted to be with her years ago, we weren't right for each other then."

"But you are now?"

"Yes, we're perfect for each other now."

"Are you going to tie the knot with her?" Beau asked.

"When she's ready."

"What if she's never ready?"

"Then I'll be happy to be with Jordan any way she lets me."

His father ambled off, leaving Beau with a heavy heart and a whole lot of thinking to do.

"You sure about this?" Beau asked Colt when he stowed his gear in the backseat of Colt's Dodge.

"Yep. By the time Ace figures out we took Midnight to Miles City, it'll be too late for him to catch us." Colt gathered up the junk on the front seat—coloring books, crayons and Happy Meal toys, then tossed them into the back. "Do me a favor and double-check the latch on the trailer."

Beau inspected the lock then hopped into the truck. "We're good to go."

As Colt pulled out of the driveway his cell phone beeped. He put the brakes on. "Better check this text in case it's Leah. Davy was running a fever last night." He looked at the message. "Shit."

"Everything okay?"

"Ace just texted 'good luck with Midnight.'"

"Doesn't surprise me. Can't pull the wool over your brother's eyes."

Colt's phone beeped again. "It's Ace. 'If Midnight gets injured you're…'"

"You're what?"

"There's a bunch of symbols and punctuation marks."

Beau grinned.

Colt lifted his foot from the brake and headed for the county road.

Sunrise was an hour away. "Any trouble loading Midnight?" Beau asked.

"Nope. The stallion practically danced his way into the trailer."

"You competing today?"

"Heck, yeah. Been looking forward to it all week."

"Need a break from married life, huh?"

"Married life is great. With Leah and the kids, there's never a dull moment."

"How's Evan?"

"He's good. Thanks for asking." Colt turned onto the highway. "He likes to Skype online so we've been doing that once a week. He's looking forward to visiting Thunder Ranch over Thanksgiving." Small talk exhausted, Colt drove in silence then swung the truck into a McDonald's on the outskirts of town and ordered two large coffees. Back on the road, he asked, "So what's up between you and Sierra?"

"Hasn't Leah gotten the latest scoop from your sister?"

"The only thing Leah mentioned after she met the girls for coffee at the diner was that Sierra seemed depressed."

When Beau remained silent, Colt said, "No comment?"

"No comment."

"Good." Colt squirmed into a comfortable position on the seat. "Now when I get home and Leah grills me on what I found out about you and Sierra, I can say 'nothing' without my face turning red."

"Why's everyone so dang interested in my love life?" Beau grumbled.

"Don't you know, cousin? No woman is happy unless all her lady friends are happy."

Exhausted from thinking about Sierra all week, Beau flipped the radio to a sports talk show.

"Okay, I can take a hint." Colt launched into a discussion about NFL teams and the drive passed quickly.

When they arrived in Miles City, Colt went off with Midnight and Beau signed in for the bull-riding event. He had time to waste before he competed, so he visited the bull pen and observed the animals for the rodeo.

He'd drawn Red Hot Chili Pepper, a brown bull with a white face. He wasn't the biggest bull in the pen but Pepper, as he was called by the cowboys, had speed and quickness on his side. Beau walked through the cowboy-ready area, then made his way toward the chutes to watch Colt compete in the saddle-bronc competition.

"Ladies and gentlemen, welcome to the Miles City Rodeo and Stock Show." When the applause died down, the announcer briefed fans on the scoring system then introduced the first contender, a cowboy from Utah who lasted five seconds before biting the dust. When Colt's name came over the sound system, Beau climbed the rails for a better view.

The gate opened and a horse named Devil's Delight

barely cleared the chute before the first buck. Beau stopped breathing when Colt slipped sideways in the saddle. His cousin managed to hang on and regain his balance. Beau counted the seconds in his head, noting the bronc went into a spin at the six-second mark. The buzzer sounded and Colt held on until he found an opening and launched himself off the horse. The crowd cheered when he came to his feet. Colt waved his hat to the fans and returned to the cowboy-ready area wearing a huge grin.

"Colt Hart sure showed Devil's Delight he was the boss!" The JumboTron replayed the ride. "The judges have spoken and Hart earned an eighty-five! Hart's the man to beat this afternoon and our next rider is sure gonna give it his best shot."

Once the fans quieted, the announcer continued. "We got a special treat up next—The Midnight Express. This stallion is a descendant of Five Minutes to Midnight, a Pro Rodeo Hall of Fame bucking horse!" The crowd cheered. "The Midnight Express disappeared from the circuit for a couple of years, but thanks to the Harts of Roundup, Montana, the stallion is back doin' what he's famous for—throwin' cowboys!"

Beau made his way over to Midnight. The horse had been loaded into the chute and Colt was helping to secure the flank strap. "Midnight has won bucking horse of the year twice and made an appearance at the National Finals Rodeo five times," the announcer said.

A cowboy, who went by the nickname Tiny Joe, hopped onto Midnight's back. The stallion stamped his hoof in anticipation. Tiny Joe bobbed his head. The chute door opened and Midnight morphed into a dark mythological warrior.

The stallion's sleek black coat and muscular stature

mesmerized rodeo fans. Midnight bucked high and tight with no letdown between kicks, and Tiny Joe didn't stand a chance past four seconds. The cowboy sailed headfirst through the air and a roar from the stands followed.

"What do you think?" Colt joined Beau.

"I'm thinking Midnight's going for broke at the Bash."

"Me, too." Colt's expression sobered. "You sure you're up to fighting a bull today?"

"I'll be fine." Beau brushed off his cousin's concern and walked away. An hour later the bull-riding competition began. Beau was third in the rotation, just enough time to get his thoughts in order and focus. Ignoring his sore ribs, he adjusted his protective vest. The livestock handlers loaded Pepper into the chute and the five-year-old bull stood docile. Beau wasn't fooled. Pepper had two years' experience on the circuit and was only biding his time until it was his turn to play.

"You're up, Adams."

Beau waited for his adrenaline to spike but his body remained oddly calm—not a good sign. He needed a rush of heat through his muscles to increase his strength. He scaled the rails and settled onto Red Hot Chili Pepper. Ignoring his subdued mood, Beau took only a few seconds to secure his grip on the rope before nodding to the gateman.

The chute opened and Pepper pounced, but Beau had anticipated the move and kept his balance. Either Beau was riding out of his head or Pepper had lost some steam, because the bull's bucks felt tame in comparison to what Midnight had put him through earlier in the week. Beau rode buck after buck as if in a daze, his ears and mind numb to the cheering crowd.

The buzzer sounded, but he kept his seat, waiting for an opening to dismount. When his chance came, he jumped for safety but his hand got hung up in the rope. Pepper continued to buck and Beau tried to reach with his free hand to loosen the rope, but it was all he could do to keep himself from falling beneath the bull and being pummeled by hooves.

The bullfighters closed in, one cowboy tugging at the rope, the other trying to distract Pepper. Beau could no longer feel his hand—the rope had cut off the circulation. Pepper spun and his rear collided with the bullfighter's horse, the impact jerking Beau's arm so hard he feared the ligaments had been torn.

Beau was running out of strength, his feet dragging against the ground. A third cowboy on horseback entered the arena and jumped into the fray. Suddenly Beau's hand broke free and his legs went out from under him. One of the bullfighters grabbed the back of Beau's jeans and hauled him away from the bucking bull then released him. Beau staggered from the arena, his arm hanging limply at his side.

"Are you all right?" Colt blocked Beau's path.

"My arm."

"C'mon, let's get you to the first-aid station."

Beau followed his cousin, feeling nauseous from the pain shooting through his injured limb. "What was my score?"

"I don't know. I didn't hear the announcer." Colt stopped at the paramedic's truck.

"Your hand got caught in the rope," the medic said. Most of the first responders watched the cowboys ride so if one of them got injured, they had some idea of what had happened.

"Might have pulled the ligaments in my shoulder," Beau said.

"While you're being looked after, I'm going to load Midnight." Colt walked off.

After an extensive examination, the medic diagnosed strained ligaments and sprained fingers. He submerged Beau's hand in a bucket of cold water and wrapped an ice pack around his shoulder, then put his arm in a sling and advised Beau to take a week or two off before riding another bull.

The ice numbed the pain but didn't prevent Sierra's face from flashing through Beau's mind. All week he'd stomped around like a bear with a sore paw because he believed Sierra hadn't cared about him the way he cared about her. But after his chat with his father last night, Beau wondered if he had jumped to the wrong conclusion.

What if Sierra kept pushing him away because she was trying to protect *him* from a future of uncertainty and challenge?

Beau was more confused than ever, except for how he felt about Sierra. He knew without a doubt that he loved her and couldn't imagine his life without her. He recalled the fight he'd gotten into with Duke this past summer. He'd wondered how the hell his brother could walk away from rodeo when the sport had been such a big part of his life and something he'd been so good at. Now he knew.

From this day forward, nothing Beau did or would do mattered if he didn't have Sierra by his side.

Chapter Fourteen

Saturday evening the diner sat empty. Sierra blamed it on the falling snow. Her aunt had retreated to the upstairs apartment with Joshua and the last customer had walked out thirty minutes ago.

"Susie," Sierra said, poking her head around the kitchen door. "I'm closing up early. Get your coat and scoot."

"Really?" Susie shrugged into her white ski jacket. "Thanks, Sierra."

"Text your parents that you're leaving work, okay?"

Susie pulled her phone from her coat pocket and a few seconds later said, "Done."

"The roads are slick." Sierra walked with her employee to the door. "Be careful."

After locking up and flipping the sign in the window, Sierra dimmed the lights and stared at the softly falling snow. A truck turned onto Main Street and her heart skipped a beat then resumed its normal rhythm when she noted the vehicle didn't belong to Beau. Her gaze shifted to Wright's Western Wear and Tack. The store's lighted display window illuminated Beau's custom-made saddles.

I miss you, Beau.

Almost a week had passed since her bungee-jumping

disaster—six miserable days of not hearing Beau's voice or seeing his handsome face. She'd believed she'd had Beau's best interests at heart, but after speaking with her aunt, she'd begun to doubt herself.

When Joshua had arrived to eat with Jordan earlier in the evening, Sierra had been tempted to ask about Beau, but she'd chickened out. A knot formed in her chest when she thought of how happy Joshua made her aunt. Even though Sierra was glad Jordan had reconnected with her old flame, she envied her aunt.

The chances of a man happening along after Sierra had lost her eyesight were zero to none—not that it mattered. She couldn't imagine sharing her life with anyone but Beau. She was destined to remain alone. With that depressing thought in mind, she returned to the kitchen and began preparations for Sunday's menu.

Sierra had lost track of time when a knock on the back door startled her. She glanced at the clock—nine-thirty. "Who's there?"

"Beau."

Sucking in a quick breath, she fumbled with the dead bolt. Beau stood in the glow of the security light, a dusting of snow covered his hat and sheepskin jacket, which hung open because of the sling around his left arm. "You're hurt." She waved him inside and shut the door. He was such a sight for sore eyes, that it took all of Sierra's strength not to throw herself at him. "What happened?"

"Strained the ligaments in my arm. Nothing a little rest won't cure."

The deep timbre of his voice sent a warm shiver down her spine. Each night she'd gone to sleep, her thoughts drifting to Beau. Eyes closed, she'd imagined him lying next to her, whispering in her ear. Lord, she'd missed the sound of his voice.

Her gaze soaked in his face, noting his split lip. "Did you get into a fight?"

He rubbed his thumb over the healing cut. "Tangled with a bronc earlier in the week."

"I thought you rode bulls."

"I ride bulls for money and broncs for fun." He smiled but stopped short of a full grin. "I went a few rounds with Midnight. We're getting him ready to compete in South Dakota on the seventeenth." He glanced around the kitchen. "Is now a good time to talk?"

"There's still coffee left in the pot. Would you like a cup?"

"No, thanks." He laid his jacket over the chair at the bistro table and set his hat on the seat, then moved closer to Sierra. "I have a few things I need to get off my chest."

Sierra swallowed hard and braced herself.

"I realize we haven't dated all that long, but I felt—" he pressed his fist to his chest "—something right here the night I found you stranded on the road outside of Roundup. That feeling became stronger each time I saw you."

She clasped her hands together, squeezing until her fingers ached.

"The news from your eye doctor wasn't what you'd hoped for. I know you believe it's changed the course of your life, but I'm here to tell you that it doesn't have to."

Blindness most definitely changed a person's life.

"I've done a lot of thinking the past few days... mostly imagining what it would be like to be married to a blind woman. I've tried to guess how the loss of your sight would impact my life…my responsibilities at Thunder Ranch.

"Don't forget your rodeo career," she said.

"At best I've got another year or two then I'll retire my bull rope."

"And what conclusion did you come to?"

He shrugged. "The only thing I know for sure is that your going blind will affect every aspect of my day-to-day life, but how much and in what ways…only time will tell."

"That's why I—"

He pressed a finger against her lips. "Then I asked myself if I could walk away from you." His finger caressed her lower lip. "The answer was no."

Sierra's breath caught in her chest.

"In the end, it doesn't matter if my plans for the future have to be altered to accommodate your blindness, because the one thing I can't live without is you." Beau cupped her cheek. "I love you, Sierra, and I don't want to spend the rest of my days on earth without you."

Her heart melted at the warmth in Beau's brown eyes.

"Let me repeat myself." He tipped her chin, forcing her to hold his gaze. "I love all of you, Sierra—the parts that work well and the parts that don't work so well."

Beau's heartfelt words made her eyes sting.

"I know I can come on too strong and I tend to take over and do things for people before they ask for my help. I can't promise that I won't smother you from time to time. But if you ask me to step back, I'll do my best to oblige."

Sierra fought valiantly to keep her tears from escaping.

"And if you are determined to do everything on your

bucket list then I won't stand in your way, but if you'll let me, I'd like to do them with you."

"Every one?" she whispered.

"Yep. I'll even take a ballroom dancing class with you." He shrugged. "I've always wanted to learn the tango."

Sierra couldn't picture the tough bull rider light on his feet. She laughed, but the sound emerged from her throat in a strangled sob.

"Loving you is the easy part," he said. "Living with your disability will be a challenge, but I'm ready and willing and eager to fight that battle." The pad of his thumb caught a tear that dribbled down her cheek.

"No matter what the future holds for you, honey, I want to be the guy walking at your side every step of the way. If you let me…if you trust me…I'll be the light in your life when your world goes dark."

"I'm afraid," she whispered.

"Of what?"

"Of becoming too dependent on you and then one day you'll wake up and realize my blindness has stolen all the joy from your life."

"That won't happen. Because I know you, Sierra Byrne. You're as stubborn and willful as your aunt and you won't let yourself become a burden to anyone."

Lord, how she loved Beau. She wanted to believe he spoke from the heart, but did she have the courage to take a leap of faith in herself? "You're not looking at the big picture. There are things I can't…won't do in the future."

"Like what?"

"I won't have children."

"Why not?"

Why was he making this so hard? "I won't have children, because I'd never risk the safety of my child."

"Why would our children be unsafe?"

Wasn't it obvious? "If I can't see where I'm going how will I see where my child is going?"

"You might not lose your sight for several years and I'd be there to help raise our kids. You wouldn't have to do it on your own."

"Good grief, Beau. Life will be difficult enough learning to run the diner when I'm blind, let alone care for children."

"You're overthinking this, Sierra."

"And you're oversimplifying it, Beau. You make raising children sound easy."

"And you make it sound impossible. The truth is probably somewhere in between." Beau kissed her mouth. "It's okay to be scared. I'm afraid, too, but not by your blindness, by the thought of not having you in my life."

"Beau, I—"

"Do you love me?"

Of course she did!

"I held you in my arms…made love to you…felt the way you loved me back." He pressed the palm of her hand against his thudding heart. "I know you love me."

Sierra didn't deny it. "It's because I love you that I refuse to take something beautiful between us and have it become ugly and hurtful in the end."

"You love me, but you won't trust me with your heart."

No, it was herself she didn't trust. "Beau, I—" What was the point? She'd already stated her case.

He reached into his pocket and removed a ring. "I came tonight to pledge my love to you and ask you to marry me. I'm not a guy that runs at the first sign of trouble, Sierra. I stick." He took her hand and slid the ring over her finger. "I picked this blue diamond because the color matches your eyes."

The ring was gorgeous. Heart pounding with love she yearned to shout, *Yes, I'll marry you!*

Beau swooped in and pressed a hard, desperate kiss to her mouth. "Don't give me your answer tonight. Wear my ring and think about the next fifty years of your life. If you can envision me and you with gray hair holding hands while our rocking chairs face west, then you have your answer."

Too choked up to speak, Sierra watched Beau fetch his coat and hat and walk out the door. Her gaze dropped to the ring on her finger. Would she stand back and allow a disease to not only rob her of her sight but also her very own happy ever after?

Or…would she find the courage to accept Beau's love?

"LADIES AND GENTLEMEN, turn your attention to chute seven." The announcer's voice boomed over the sound system Saturday afternoon at the Badlands Bull Bash and Cowboy Stampede in Spearfish, South Dakota.

Beau ignored the hoopla and spoke to Colt. "You ready?"

"I'd better be or I'll disappoint our cheering section."

Beau followed Colt's gaze. Except for Dinah, who'd remained behind to safeguard the citizens of Roundup, the entire family had made the five-hour drive to the rodeo, even Flynn, whose due date was less than two weeks away.

After Colt walked over to his chute, Duke said, "Dad's still not here."

"I hope he doesn't miss Midnight's performance." Earlier that day after Beau had hit the road with Back Bender and Bushwhacker, his father had called to tell him that Jordan had forgotten something in Roundup and they'd be late to the rodeo.

"Any sign of your dad?" Ace asked.

"Nope. And he's not answering his phone," Beau said.

"You don't think they had car trouble, do you?" Austin joined the group.

Ace shook his head. "Uncle Joshua would have phoned Mom if something serious had happened."

"Up next is the final ride in the saddle-bronc competition," the announcer said. "Colt Hart from Roundup, Montana, will be ridin' King of Spades—a two-time national champion bronc!"

Ace, Duke, Austin and Beau approached the chute where Colt prepared for his ride. King of Spades had a reputation of rallying in the final seconds and throwing his rider. Duke and Ace made sure the rigging was adjusted properly while Colt played with his grip on the rope.

A few seconds later Colt signaled the gateman. The moment King of Spades entered the arena he kicked high and followed the move with a tight spin that would have thrown a seasoned cowboy into the stands. Colt held on and the crowd cheered its approval.

"He's slipping," Beau said when Colt's butt shifted sideways. *Four...five...*

"Hang on, Colt!" Ace shouted.

Six...seven...

The buzzer sounded and not a second too soon. Colt went flying over the bronc's head but managed to tuck his body and roll when he landed.

"I'll be darned! Colt Hart is the first cowboy to make it to eight this season on King of Spades!"

Colt got to his feet and saluted the crowd.

"Hart scored an eighty-seven! That's good enough for first place."

Beau glanced at his family cheering in the stands, wishing Sierra sat among them. He felt like the odd man out…all his cousins had special ladies in their lives and Beau wished Sierra was his. He'd poured his heart out to her two weeks ago, but feared he'd come up short. The only thing giving him hope was that she hadn't returned his ring.

"Rodeo fans sit back and get ready for the next event of the day—bareback ridin'!"

"Midnight's turn to shine." Duke watched Ace lead Midnight into his chute. The stallion didn't balk, as if he sensed his behavior and performance would determine his rodeo future.

When Colt returned to the cowboy-ready area, Beau congratulated Colt on his win. "You're a hard act to follow, cousin."

Duke and Austin slapped Colt on the back.

"Is this the famed Midnight?" The question arrived before the cowboy.

Beau shoved his elbow into Colt's side. "Keep your eye on Kendall. He's got a reputation for provoking horses in the chute." Beau had run into Wesley Kendall over the summer and wherever the cowboy went controversy followed.

Kendall climbed the rails and raised his arm in the air as if preparing to slap Midnight on the head. Ace's hand shot out, blocking Kendall's arm. "Watch yourself, cowboy."

"Just playin' with him." Kendall sneered. "Can't

blame me for wantin' to rile him when he stands there like a docile mare."

Ace leveled a hard stare at Kendall and the cowboy walked off. "I'm watching Midnight from the stands." Ace pointed to Kendall's buddies standing nearby. "Make sure no one gets within ten feet of this chute."

"I'll check Kendall's spurs to see if the rowels turn freely," Colt said before Ace walked away.

"Rodeo fans, we've got a great group of broncs for our bareback competition!"

Midnight and Kendall were up last, and each time Kendall wandered closer to the chute, Beau and Austin blocked his path. Beau was torn between wanting Kendall to get thrown on his ass at the one-second mark and wanting him to go six or seven seconds on Midnight before being thrown, so the judges got a sense of the stallion's real talent.

"Out of my way, Adams." Kendall made a move toward the chute but Duke and Colt closed ranks with Beau and Austin, preventing Kendall from passing. A stare-down ensued. Finally Kendall backed off and waited until the announcer called his name.

"Ladies and gentlemen, the final ride in the bareback competition pairs Wesley Kendall from Sioux City, South Dakota, and The Midnight Express, the famed offspring of Five Minutes to Midnight—a Pro Rodeo Hall of Fame bucker!"

The crowd erupted in applause. After Kendall had hopped onto Midnight's back, Colt climbed the rails and reached for the cowboy's boot.

Kendall jerked his foot away. "What the hell are you doing, Hart?"

"Checking to make sure your spurs are legal." Colt spun the spur, satisfied the tips were blunt.

"Sit back and cry, Hart, 'cause this so-called famous horse your family owns is going to bite the dust." Kendall adjusted the rope around his hand then signaled the gateman.

Beau didn't know who was more surprised when Midnight shot out of the chute like a bullet—the gateman who scrambled to get out of the way or Kendall who almost lost his seat. Midnight's first buck was high and tight, interfering with Kendall's spurring rhythm. The stallion added a spin, which threw Kendall off balance at the four-second mark. The cowboy fought to stay alive, but Midnight showed no mercy. His bucks proved too powerful for Kendall and the cowboy flew off. Midnight continued to buck, adding insult to injury when he stomped on Kendall's hat. The fans came to their feet, roaring their approval.

Beau, Colt, Austin and Duke met Midnight when he was escorted from the arena. The dang stallion pranced as if he'd just won a world title. Colt whispered to the stallion and Midnight settled down, allowing Colt to walk him to the livestock area.

A few minutes later Beau's aunt, his father and Ace met them at Midnight's stall.

"He was amazing," Aunt Sarah said.

"Haven't seen a horse perform like that in years," Beau's father chimed in.

"What do you all think?" Colt asked. "Is Midnight ready to make a run for another NFR title?"

"After that performance, I agree that it would be a shame to allow his talent to go to waste," Ace said.

Colt patted Midnight's rump. "You hear that, big guy? You're going on the road next year!"

Beau tugged his father's sleeve. "Everything okay with you and Jordan?"

"Meant to get here sooner but we had to go back to town and pick up something."

"What did you forget?" Beau asked.

His father and Aunt Sarah stepped aside to reveal Sierra standing a few yards away. Beau's knees went weak when she flashed him a hesitant smile. "We'll be watching you from the stands, Beau," Duke said. "Good luck with your ride."

His family walked off, leaving him alone with Sierra. Beau's gaze dropped to her hand and his heart thudded hard at the sight of the diamond ring on her finger. He was riding in less than a half hour—no time to beat around the bush. "You're wearing my ring."

"I may not have any choice when it comes to losing my eyesight but I do have a choice who I want to spend the rest of my life with."

"You're choosing me?"

"I love you, Beau, and yes, I want to spend the rest of my life with you."

"As my wife?"

"As your wife and God willing as the mother of your children."

He grasped her hands and squeezed gently. "Once you say *I do* there's no turning back."

"I don't want to spend the rest of my life regretting that I didn't have the courage to trust in our love for one another."

Beau wrapped his arms around Sierra and for the first time in fourteen days he felt as if he could take a deep breath without his chest pinching. "You've made me the happiest man alive."

"I'll ask one more time and then I'll never ask again," she said. "Are you sure, Beau? Really sure?"

"Honey, I'm a bull rider. I live for challenges."

"But marrying me will last a lot longer than eight seconds—I hope."

"No worries, darlin'. Marriage to you is one ride I refuse to get thrown from." Beau ignored the rowdy whistles of the cowboys nearby when Sierra threw her arms around his neck and kissed him.

They pulled apart and Beau grinned. "I didn't see that comin'."

"You didn't see…and here I thought I was the one who had vision issues."

The announcer introduced the bull-riding event, and Beau said, "I've gotta head over to the chutes to watch the Thunder Ranch bulls compete."

"Beau?"

"Yeah, babe?"

"Win."

"I'm feeling pretty lucky right now." He chuckled. "Think I'll go on out there and do like you say…win." Sierra's impending blindness was all the motivation Beau needed to perform his best, not only today but next season when he went after the national title. Rodeo was a tough sport and there were no guarantees he'd remain injury-free and make it to the NFR, but it sure would be special if Sierra was able to see him ride in Vegas. He considered the grueling rodeo schedule, and being away from Sierra, and decided next year would definitely be his last run at a title.

"C'mon, I'll walk you to the stands."

Sierra's feet remained planted. "If this is going to work between us then you have to let me do things on my own."

Backing down was going to be difficult, but Beau was determined to do his best. "Okay, but I have a few conditions of my own."

"Oh?"

"The next extreme activity you engage in had better be with me—" he lowered his voice "—in our bedroom." He kissed her mouth then said, "Be careful."

She walked off but stopped suddenly and looked over her shoulder. "Don't stand there and watch me. Go on."

Stubborn gal. Beau turned away and strolled several yards before checking over his shoulder. Sierra remained in the same spot staring at him. He couldn't take his eyes off her as he kept walking…right into another cowboy.

After apologizing he glanced at Sierra, and sure enough she was laughing. She shook her head and left, making her way through the maze of cowboys and gear bags littering the ground.

Beau stopped outside Bushwhacker's chute, glad to see the bull appeared his usual calm self. Bushwhacker's good manners in the chute fooled most cowboys, leaving them unprepared when the gate opened.

"Folks, cowboy Leif Rimsky will kick off the bull-riding event. Rimsky's from Albuquerque, New Mexico, and had a good year up until July when he busted his arm. The bone's healed and Rimsky's ready to ride Bushwhacker from the Thunder Ranch in Roundup, Montana. This bull's makin' a name for himself and odds are you'll see him at the NFR in Vegas, if not this year then next."

C'mon, Bushwhacker, go out there and show 'em what you've got.

Rimsky fussed with the bull rope, then a second later the chute door opened and Bushwhacker took off, his back legs kicking before he'd even cleared the chute. The bull's muscles rippled and bunched with each powerful burst of energy. Rimsky managed to hang on until

Bushwhacker twisted his hind quarters, the movement forcing Rimsky off balance. The cowboy made a futile attempt to regain his seat but in the end he went flying. The bullfighters closed in, distracting Bushwhacker who continued to entertain the crowd with his powerful kicks.

"Looks like Bushwhacker will remain undefeated this year!" The crowd cheered when the JumboTron replayed Rimsky's ride.

Once Bushwhacker was led from the arena and safely returned to the bull pen, Beau located Back Bender. The bull appeared agitated, slamming his hoof against the chute. Beau moved closer and climbed the rails, checking to make sure the rigging was properly secured. Satisfied, Beau chalked up the bull's testiness to an eagerness to rid himself of the cowboy on his back.

The gate opened and Back Bender jumped into action. He spun right then left, ending with a double kick that dislodged the rider. Back Bender continued to buck and it took the bullfighters a good thirty seconds to guide the animal out of the arena.

Happy that Midnight and the bulls had represented Thunder Ranch well, Beau put on his protective vest and headgear. He was next in the rotation and adrenaline was pumping hard through his veins.

"Ladies and gentlemen, it's been a day of hits and misses for the cowboys here at the Bash. We got one ride left and it's a doozy!"

Beau engaged in an all-out battle with his brain to remain focused and not think about how happy Sierra had made him. He'd drawn Blood Sucker, a bull from the Jeopardy Ranch in Idaho. Blood Sucker was a money bull and didn't often allow a cowboy to ride him for eight seconds.

Right now, Blood Sucker appeared none too pleased to be confined to his chute. The bull threw his side against the rails, forcing one cowboy to jump for safety before he got his foot smashed. When Beau settled on Blood Sucker's back, an image of Sierra flashed through his mind and he felt a sense of peace. Making sure his grip was secure, he relaxed his spine and leaned forward.

The gate burst open and the bull jumped into the arena with a fierce one-two kick that put a whole lotta daylight between Beau's butt and the bull. He clenched his thigh muscles against the bull's girth, which helped him regain his balance. His left arm burned with pain, the newly healed ligaments stretching and pulling against their will.

One more second, that's all he needed. Just…one…more…

The buzzer sounded and the raucous cheering encouraged Beau to hang on through another series of vicious bucks. Satisfied he'd made an impression, Beau released the rope and dove for safety. He came to his feet and applause echoed through the stands.

"Well, folks, there you have it. Tonight's winning bull ride! Beau Adams scored an eighty-six on Blood Sucker—the highest score to date on that bull. Congratulations, cowboy!"

An hour later, Beau, Duke, Ace, Colt and Austin had loaded the Thunder Ranch bulls into the stock trailer and were preparing to load Midnight when Kendall walked by and clanged his gear against the side of the trailer. The sharp noise startled Midnight and he reared. Ace moved in on one side and Colt on the other, grabbing the ropes attached to the halter. When Midnight came down, his left front leg missed the ramp and he stumbled.

"Whoa, Midnight, whoa," Colt said.

By the time the stallion settled down, Kendall was nowhere in sight.

"Don't load him." Ace crouched next to Midnight and examined the knee joint then groaned.

"What is it?" Duke asked.

"He twisted his knee. It's swelling already."

"Here." Colt handed the ropes to Duke then looked at Austin. "Post my bail if I end up in the slammer for killing Kendall."

Beau blocked Colt's path. "Leave him be. He can't avoid us forever. He'll meet up with me on the road sooner or later."

"I want to put ice on Midnight's knee before we load him." Ace stood. "Be be right back."

"Great. Just frickin' great. Midnight makes a name for himself and now this." Colt whipped off his hat and banged it against his thigh.

"Ace'll fix Midnight," Duke said.

Colt shook his head. "What if it's more than a bruised knee?"

"One day at a time, cousin," Beau stroked Midnight's neck. "Right now let's pamper this big guy and enjoy his victory."

Thunder Ranch had come out the big winner today and the future looked promising, especially for Beau now that he'd be joining the rest of the men in the family and tying the knot with the woman of his dreams.

Epilogue

Thanksgiving at Thunder Ranch was a big production. The scents of rosemary, sage and roasting turkeys filled the house. Casserole dishes lined the kitchen countertops and cooling pies sat on the windowsill. Aunt Sarah, Angie, Leah and Austin's sister, Cheyenne, hustled about the kitchen putting the finishing touches on the meal.

Beau hovered in the doorway, waiting for an opportunity to steal a piece of meat from the two birds Earl McKinley had been instructed to carve. A third bird cooked outside in the deep fryer.

"Don't even think about it, Beau," his aunt warned him. "When is Duke getting here?"

"Around three o'clock. He said to keep a plate warming in the oven." Duke had volunteered to take the day shift after Aunt Sarah had invited Austin's father, Buddy, and Cheyenne and her twin girls to join the family. Dinah, Austin and Buddy had just left the house to go visit Midnight.

Beau wandered down the hall to investigate the shouting coming from the family room. Sierra was playing a video game with Colt's son, Evan, and by her excited voice Beau assumed she was beating the poor kid. Who would have believed his fiancée was a closet gamer?

While Leah's kids, Davy and Jill, were sprawled on the floor with Cheyenne's twins, Sadie and Sammie, engrossed in a board game, Flynn sat on the couch with her sock feet resting on the coffee table, listening to Luke read a book. Flynn's baby was due in seven days and her pinched expression conveyed how miserable and uncomfortable she was.

"Uncle Beau?" Luke said.

"What, kid?"

"Look." Luke propped the book on Flynn's huge stomach. "It stays open all by itself."

Flynn rolled her eyes.

"Hey, Flynn, where's Ace and Colt?" Beau asked.

"In the barn with Midnight."

Midnight's bruised knee was healing, the swelling almost completely gone. Since the Badlands Bull Bash, Aunt Sarah had received several calls from ranchers interested in breeding their mares with Midnight, giving the family hope that things were finally turning around for the ranch. No one had wanted to jinx Midnight's recovery by talking about the stallion competing for an NFR title next year, but Beau suspected it was on everyone's mind.

"Hey! How'd you do that?" Evan grinned at Sierra. The kid was the spitting image of Colt but remained shy around the family.

"Watch and weep, kid." Sierra pointed the controller at the large-screen TV mounted to the wall and captured three of Evan's alien commandos. Before Sierra could gloat too much, the front door banged open and boots clomped down the hall. Colt entered the room and Jill and Davy practically tripped over themselves as they raced to their stepfather, scampering up his legs and into his arms.

"Hey, Evan, get one of these pesky bugs off me, will you?"

Evan grinned at his father's predicament. "Sorry, you're on your own. I'm about to take control of planet Zorcon."

"You and what army?" Sierra said. "Bingo! You're dead."

"Ah, man!" Evan set aside his controller and approached Colt. Jill immediately held out her arms. "Take me, Evan! Take me!"

Watching how well Colt's kids got along made Beau eager to have children with Sierra. She must have sensed his thoughts because her gaze connected with his from across the room. Each time Beau lost himself in her beautiful blue eyes, he was reminded of all the uncertainties they faced in the future. Even so, he wasn't worried. Having Sierra in his life made him appreciate each day and the small blessings that came his way.

"Beau?" Aunt Sarah called from the kitchen.

"You summoned?" he said, when he entered the room.

"I told your father not to stand so close to the turkey fryer, but he refuses to listen."

It wasn't like Aunt Sarah to be short-tempered and Beau suspected her frazzled mood had to do with Tuf not being present on a day meant for family gatherings. She had to be hurting that her youngest son continued to keep his distance from the family.

"Please go out there and say something before your father knocks the fryer over and burns down the house."

When Beau stepped onto the patio he found his father and Jordan bundled in their winter coats, hugging each other. "Hey, Dad." The cozy couple broke apart. "Aunt Sarah says you're standing too close to the fryer."

"I've been the designated turkey fryer for the past ten years. I know what I'm doing."

"She's worried one of you might get burned."

"My sister worries too much."

Jordan moved away from the fryer, tugging Joshua's coat sleeve until he followed. "Beau," Jordan spoke. "Have you and Sierra set a wedding date?"

"Not yet." If Beau had any say in the matter, they'd marry right now in a civil ceremony at Thunder Ranch, but Sierra wanted to remain engaged for a little while. He suspected she worried that he'd change his mind about marrying her, but he was a determined man and sooner or later she'd figure out he wasn't going anywhere without her. "Are you in a hurry to see us married off?"

"We were hoping you'd wed sooner rather than later," his father said.

"Why?" Beau grinned. "Do you two want to tie the knot?"

His father's expression turned pensive.

Worried he'd overstepped his bounds, Beau mumbled, "Sorry. I didn't mean to—"

Jordan held out her left hand, showing off a small diamond solitaire on her ring finger.

"You got engaged. Congratulations."

"No," his father said. "We got married."

Shocked, Beau asked, "When?"

"On the way home from South Dakota. We stayed the night in Billings while the rest of you returned to Roundup."

Jordan smiled up at Joshua. "We'd rather not tell

anyone we're married until after you and Sierra tie the knot."

"Why?"

"I want all the excitement and focus to be on your wedding," Jordan said.

That might be difficult when the Harts and the Adams were procreating like rabbits. Beau was betting a new baby would be born every year for the next decade.

"As soon as you and Sierra are married, Jordan's moving into the house with me," his father said.

"Joshua and I thought you wouldn't mind living in the apartment above the diner until you and Sierra decide where you want to settle permanently."

"Sure. I guess that would be okay." Beau hadn't given any thought to where he and Sierra would live. It made sense for them to stay in town since Sierra ran the diner.

Feeling chilled from standing outside without a coat, Beau pointed to the fryer. "Watch yourself. Aunt Sarah's stressed out today."

"Every holiday is hard on her without Tuf," his father said.

When Beau entered the house all hell had broken loose. Aunt Sarah and Earl were racing around the kitchen covering the food dishes with aluminum foil.

"What happened?" Beau asked.

"It's Flynn. Her water broke. We're going to the hospital," Aunt Sarah said.

Beau rushed to the family room where Colt was helping Flynn into her coat.

"Did anyone tell Ace?" Beau asked.

"The kids ran out to the barn to get him," Colt said.

A moment later, the front door opened. "Where is she?" Ace yelled.

"I'm right here, Ace." Flynn waddled into the hall.

"It's too early," Ace insisted, his eyes pleading with his wife.

"Calm down, honey." Aunt Sarah grabbed her jacket from the hall closet. "Women have babies every day. Flynn will be fine."

"Where's my purse?" Flynn asked.

Earl retrieved the purse from the floor next to the couch in the family room and took it to his daughter.

"Thanks, Dad." She kissed his cheek. "Don't look so worried."

"What about all the food?" Beau asked when everyone put on their coats. His question startled the group and all eyes turned to Aunt Sarah.

"Earl and I will go with Flynn and Ace. The rest of you stay here and eat. We'll keep you posted from the hospital."

Ace ushered Flynn out the door, and Earl and Aunt Sarah followed. The rest of the family stood in the hallway staring at one another. The back door opened and Beau's father yelled, "The deep-fried turkey's ready!"

The pronouncement set the women in motion and the kids raced back into the family room. The men retired to the living room to pour themselves a drink and wager whether or not Flynn would have a girl or a boy.

Beau and Sierra were left standing in the hallway alone. He gathered her in his arms. "Are you ready to join this family? There's never a dull moment around here."

"You and all the chaos your family brings is exactly what I need in my life." Sierra caressed his cheek. "I love you, Beau."

He kissed Sierra, trying to convey without words

how much she meant to him. When they broke apart, he said, "I'm going to need a lot more practice doing that."

"Doing what?"

"Showing you how much I love you."

This time Sierra initiated the kiss, and when it ended, she whispered, "I don't need to look into your eyes to *see* how much you love me. I feel it right here." She pressed Beau's hand to her heart, which pounded hard and steady.

"I know what I want for Christmas."

"What's that?" she asked.

"For you to set a wedding date." He nuzzled her neck.

"I might even do better than that."

"Oh?"

"If you play your cards right, Mr. Adams, you just might wake up Christmas morning in my bed."

"Now that would be a Christmas present this cowboy would never forget."

* * * * *

Be sure to look for
TOMAS: COWBOY HOMECOMING
by Linda Warren, the last book in the
HARTS OF THE RODEO *miniseries,*
available in December 2012!

REQUEST YOUR FREE BOOKS!
2 FREE NOVELS PLUS 2 FREE GIFTS!

♠ Harlequin®

American ★ Romance®

LOVE, HOME & HAPPINESS

YES! Please send me 2 FREE Harlequin® American Romance® novels and my 2 FREE gifts (gifts are worth about $10). After receiving them, if I don't wish to receive any more books, I can return the shipping statement marked "cancel." If I don't cancel, I will receive 4 brand-new novels every month and be billed just $4.49 per book in the U.S. or $5.24 per book in Canada. That's a saving of at least 14% off the cover price! It's quite a bargain! Shipping and handling is just 50¢ per book in the U.S. and 75¢ per book in Canada.* I understand that accepting the 2 free books and gifts places me under no obligation to buy anything. I can always return a shipment and cancel at any time. Even if I never buy another book, the two free books and gifts are mine to keep forever.

154/354 HDN FEP2

Name _____ (PLEASE PRINT)

Address _____ Apt. #

City _____ State/Prov. _____ Zip/Postal Code

Signature (if under 18, a parent or guardian must sign)

Mail to the **Reader Service:**
IN U.S.A.: P.O. Box 1867, Buffalo, NY 14240-1867
IN CANADA: P.O. Box 609, Fort Erie, Ontario L2A 5X3

Not valid for current subscribers to Harlequin American Romance books.

Want to try two free books from another line?
Call 1-800-873-8635 or visit www.ReaderService.com.

* Terms and prices subject to change without notice. Prices do not include applicable taxes. Sales tax applicable in N.Y. Canadian residents will be charged applicable taxes. Offer not valid in Quebec. This offer is limited to one order per household. All orders subject to credit approval. Credit or debit balances in a customer's account(s) may be offset by any other outstanding balance owed by or to the customer. Please allow 4 to 6 weeks for delivery. Offer available while quantities last.

Your Privacy—The Reader Service is committed to protecting your privacy. Our Privacy Policy is available online at www.ReaderService.com or upon request from the Reader Service.

We make a portion of our mailing list available to reputable third parties that offer products we believe may interest you. If you prefer that we not exchange your name with third parties, or if you wish to clarify or modify your communication preferences, please visit us at www.ReaderService.com/consumerschoice or write to us at Reader Service Preference Service, P.O. Box 9062, Buffalo, NY 14269. Include your complete name and address.

HARI1B

ROMANTIC
SUSPENSE

Get your heart racing this holiday season with double the pulse-pounding action.

Christmas Confidential

Featuring

Holiday Protector by **Marilyn Pappano**

Miri Duncan doesn't care that it's almost Christmas. She's got bigger worries on her mind. But surviving the trip to Georgia from Texas is going to be her biggest challenge. Days in a car with the man who broke her heart and helped send her to prison—private investigator Dean Montgomery.

A Chance Reunion by **Linda Conrad**

When the husband Elana Novak left behind five years ago shows up in her new California home she knows danger is coming her way. To protect the man she is quickly falling for Elana must convince private investigator Gage Chance that she is a different person. But Gage isn't about to let her walk away…even with the bad guys right on their heels.

Available December 2012 wherever books are sold!

The Bowman siblings have avoided Christmas ever since a family tragedy took the lives of their parents during the holiday years ago. But twins Trace and Taft Bowman have gotten past their grief, courtesy of the new women in their lives. Is it sister Caidy's turn to find love—perhaps with the new veterinarian in town?

*Read on for an excerpt from
A COLD CREEK NOEL by USA TODAY
bestselling author RaeAnne Thayne, next in her
ongoing series THE COWBOYS OF COLD CREEK*

***

"For what it's worth, I think the guys around here are crazy. Even if you did grow up with them."

He might have left things at that, safe and uncomplicated, except his eyes suddenly shifted to her mouth and he didn't miss the flare of heat in her gaze. He swore under his breath, already regretting what he seemed to have no power to resist, and then he reached for her.

As his mouth settled over hers, warm and firm and tasting of cocoa, Caidy couldn't quite believe this was happening.

She was being kissed by the sexy new veterinarian, just a day after thinking him rude and abrasive. For a long moment she was shocked into immobility, then heat began to seep through her frozen stupor. Oh. Oh, yes!

How long had it been since she had enjoyed a kiss and wanted more? She was astounded to realize she couldn't really remember. As his lips played over hers, she shifted her neck slightly for a better angle. Her insides seemed to give a collective shiver. Mmm. This was exactly what two people ought to be doing at 3:00 a.m. on a cold December day.

He made a low sound in his throat that danced down her spine, and she felt the hard strength of his arms slide around her, pulling her closer. In this moment, nothing else seemed to matter but Ben Caldwell and the wondrous sensations fluttering through her.

Still, this was crazy. Some tiny voice of self-preservation seemed to whisper through her. What was she doing? She had no business kissing someone she barely knew and wasn't even sure she liked yet.

Though it took every last ounce of strength, she managed to slide away from all that delicious heat and move a few inches away from him, trying desperately to catch her breath.

The distance she created between them seemed to drag Ben back to his senses. He stared at her, his eyes looking as dazed as she felt. "That was wrong. I don't know what I was thinking. Your dog is a patient and…I shouldn't have…"

She might have been offended by the dismay in his voice if not for the arousal in his eyes. But his hair was a little rumpled and he had the evening shadow of a beard and all she could think was *yum*.

***

Can Caidy and Ben put their collective pasts behind them and find a brilliant future together?

Find out in A COLD CREEK NOEL, coming in December 2012 from Harlequin Special Edition. And coming in 2013, also from Harlequin Special Edition, look for Ridge's story….